Northbound

by

Stuart F. Griffin

A Story of Circumstances
that Changed People's Lives.
Some for Good, Some for Evil,
but No One Remained the Same.

ASPECT Books

www.ASPECTBooks.com

Copyright © 2011 Stuart F. Griffin
ISBN-13: 978-1-57258-710-6 (Paperback)
ISBN-13: 978-1-57258-711-3 (ePub)
ISBN-13: 978-1-57258-826-4 (Kindle/Mobi)
Library of Congress Control Number: 2011908334

Published by

ASPECT Books

www.ASPECTBooks.com

Dedication

To my dear wife, Lois, for her patience and encouragement during the time of writing this book.

To Merina Thompson for her knowledge and hard work in editing the pages of this book.

Also to Celeste Perrino Walker who, through her technical support and advice, greatly helped in the completion of this book.

My final words of thanks and dedication are to my Lord Jesus Christ who gave His life for me and also gave me the idea for this book.

Table of Contents

Chapter One

The Scare of His Life

The sun had just broken through the trees, making the wet leaves reflect the light of the sun as if they had grown diamonds. *It's always amazing the way God can take the simplest of things and make them beautiful,* mused Sheriff Will Jacobs as he saddled Bella, his roan mare.

Nature had always intrigued him, making him appreciate God's love and care. He called California home, and to him it was the finest landscape he had ever seen. The ocean lying to the west, the desert, the large stands of timber to the north, the Sierra Nevada mountain range, and an abundance of fertile soil—all added to the beauty of the West.

Bella shifted away from him as he tightened the girth, and he laid a hand on her withers. "Steady," he said. The horse stood almost 17 hands high. After a night of rest, she was fresh and eager to move on. Will cinched his bedroll to the back of his saddle. The sun felt warm on his face, and he was grateful for it. He was damp and cold from having nothing but his bedroll between him and the ground. As he mounted Bella and rode off, he noticed the recent rain had made the trail slippery in spots, and he guided his horse to firmer terrain.

The sheriff hoped to be home by noon—it was possible if he pushed hard. He looked forward to seeing his wife, Emma, and his little girl, Loretta.

Emma will be pleased to know that I did not take the marshall's job, he thought to himself. She loved the town of Stone Ridge because she had roots there.

Two years earlier, in 1851, they'd bought a small house on the north end of town. He and Emma worked well together. With her touch as a homemaker and his carpentry skills, the house slowly took shape and become a home. The townspeople had accepted them, and Emma had made friends who were important to her. She was particularly close to Elizabeth, and Elizabeth's daughter, Molly, was Loretta's favorite playmate.

By and large, a wide variety of people called Stone Ridge home, many settling there after the long migration West. Those that migrated came with some sort of emotional problems that manifested itself in one way or another. Traveling West was filled with heartache and disappointment. But it was the growth in crime that gave the sheriff his greatest concern.

With the discovery of gold up north came the fever to get rich quick, which made the towns and mining camps grow at an unstoppable pace. Stony, as some had nicknamed it, had inherited some of this gold money along the way. But prosperity had its hooks, and at times, it penetrated deep into the soul. Some men seemed to be willing to do anything to turn over a new dollar.

Will tried to understand this deep hunger for gold, a hunger that would make a man leave his wife and children in search for it. Then if they found it, some would lie, cheat, and sometimes kill to hold on to the precious "yellow" they had acquired. At times he wished he had the ability to know the intent of a man's heart, but that could be more of a curse than a blessing, for the hidden things of the heart are known only by God.

Then there were the drifters who were cut from a different mold. A few decided to stay and start a new life; the rest just moved on with their restless hearts, still in search of what they had not yet found.

Carl Muller was one such man. He had drifted into town a year earlier. Muller often got drunk, but one dreadful day he killed a man and wounded another over a card game at the saloon. He had then stepped into the street yelling, "Sheriff Jacobs, face me! Do you hear me?"

The sheriff had never met a man more vile than Carl Muller. He was the kind of man who didn't care for anyone or anything, not even himself. The sheriff still had misgivings over having to shoot him. But Muller had left him no other choice.

As Bella pushed through some dried brush crowding in on the trail, Will was a bit surprised to see Dry Creek so soon. They were making good time. He patted the horse's neck, and she shook her mane, dislodging several deer flies. The creek was swollen more than he had expected; the rain had definitely fallen harder here.

"Bella, this creek could be trouble for us." She shook her head as if she understood the words. He decided to travel downstream a number of yards to find a more suitable place to cross that was shallower.

He paused near the edge of the creek and the location he had selected to cross at. "We can walk or ride through it, but I'd rather ride, girl. It would keep my boots dryer you know." As he was crossing over, he noticed spring flowers on the opposite bank that reminded him of Emma—she loved flowers.

"Sheriff Jacobs!" A man's voice cut sharply through his thoughts. A rider careened down the trail toward him on a lathered horse. Reining up, he sent a shower of stones as the horse sank onto its haunches and slid to an abrupt halt, heaving and snorting.

Will could feel his guts twist with a strong sense of apprehension. "Buckley! What's the trouble?" John Buckley was not a man prone to needless haste—something had clearly gone wrong in his absence.

Will kicked Bella, urging her across the last of the creek. When she reached the bank, she lunged up it toward the well-worn trail to meet the rider of bad news. He could see Buckley was pale and agitated. "It's Emma; she gone! She's been kidnapped!"

"Kidnapped? Emma? When?" Will demanded.

"Two days ago from your house!" Buckley replied tersely.

Will felt a sudden sickness wash over him. Without waiting to hear anymore, Will spurred Bella, slapping her with the ends of the reins and urging her on. He leaned over her neck and felt her hoof beats match the pounding of his heart. His thoughts raced. *Emma! Kidnapped! Why would anyone do such a thing? What could they hope to accomplish? Why was Buckley sent two days late?* No answers came.

He wasn't paying any attention to the muddy and slippery trail until Bella's flying hooves slipped out from under her, and they almost went down in a heap. A quick jerk upward on the reins averted disaster, and the mare regained her footing, but he noticed foam flecking her sides. Reluctantly he slowed her to a more reasonable pace, but fear gripped his mind like a trap holding its prey. His life, and the life of his family, would never be the same again. They had turned a corner, and he couldn't see where it was leading.

Will continued to ride for town. He had forgotten about Buckley, who was working hard to keep up. Suddenly he heard his traveling companion's voice in the distance. "Sheriff! Watch the ridge; it's hazardous like the trail!"

Will knew he was right. As they topped the ridge, Will didn't notice the fine view that looked north to town with the shops on the main street or the trees that spread their branches like the wings of a bird to shade the passerby from the noonday sun. There were the side streets that the sheriff walked on his rounds, which were lined with homes and places to rent. Families and singles, young and old lived and worked on and around these streets.

Will rode down the ridge and toward town. As he reached the outskirts, he picked up speed again, now that Bella had sure footing. It was midweek, which always brought an increase of life to the pulse of the town. The main street was alive with the sounds of the blacksmith's hammer, wagons, horses, and the ringing of a small bell on the door of a shop as customers came or went. The mud was a strong reminder of the hard rain. But mud could be a blessing if viewed in the right way because it kept the dust down for a short time.

Will dismounted and tied his horse to the post. Buckley suddenly pulled up beside him. "I'll water and wipe her down quickly for you," he said.

"Don't be gone long because I'm heading out soon!" he replied as he moved toward his office door. Henry Peterson, his only deputy, looked up to see Will coming through the door. Peterson quickly stood up and walked to the front of the desk to greet him. "I'm glad your back, Will!"

Will nodded his head in response. "Peterson, tell me everything you know, and don't leave out any details!"

"I don't have a lot to tell you. Emma took Loretta to play with Abe's daughter, and then she returned to your place. That was Monday morning. Abe's wife, Elizabeth, told me that Emma was going to get some things done while Loretta and Molly played. That's when they abducted her."

"How many took her?" Will said abruptly, wiping the sweat from his forehead.

"The tracks show two men, and they went in the back door. It looks like they caught her in the bedroom. There were a few things broken on the floor. The bed had been moved, and the dresser was rummaged through, just like the rest of the house. The men were looking for something. Do you have any idea what that could be, Will?"

"No! We don't hide things from each other! I'll survey the house before I ride out. But there has to be more clues than that," he said loudly.

"Will, I have a few things left to tell you," Peterson responded, trying to conceal his feelings of edginess.

"Did the men come into town? Did anyone see them? Did anyone see anything?" Will asked as he felt impatience welling up in him.

"No, Will! All the signs indicate that everything happened at your place, and then they headed north. I sent men out after them—Buckley, Wilkes, Morrison, and a few others. Buckley came back early and gave me a report. The rest of the men came back last night with nothing new to report. Did Buckley tell you much?"

"No, I didn't give him much of a chance!"

Peterson continued, "After they left with Emma, they followed the creek to its head, then over Watt's Mountain to the main road. Buckley and the others lost their tracks when they hit the main road."

Will looked Peterson square in the eye and said, "Why did you wait so long to send Buckley after me?"

"I thought, Will, seeing the kind of man you are, you'd be back as soon as you could. I regret letting you down."

Will felt his temper take hold. "Peterson! This is Emma we're talking about here. These men have two days on me and then some! They have my wife! But I don't have time to squabble with you over this, and how they lost the tracks once they hit the road, I can't figure!"

Will picked up some things from around the office and stated, "You're going to need a deputy. The town is in your hands now. I'll be back, but God only knows when. Talk to Ben Frost; he'll take care of the needed details for you."

"Good luck, Will," Peterson said.

"I need the good Lord's help, not good luck, Peterson. Don't get yourself killed," Will said as he slammed the door behind him.

As Will stepped outside, he saw Abe, Elizabeth, Molly, and his little girl. Loretta, seeing her father, ran to him saying "Daddy! Daddy!" Will reached down and took her in his arms and said, "Honey, I missed you."

"Daddy, where's Mommy? I don't know where she is!" Will held her tight as he kissed away a few of her tears.

"Honey, I'm going to go get Mommy now, and we'll be back as soon as we can."

"Daddy! Why did she go away?" Loretta asked, her wet eyes pleading with his for answers.

"Mommy had to go away for a little while, Honey. I want you to stay with Molly and Mr. and Mrs. McNeil until Mommy and I get back."

"Daddy, I don't want to stay here! I want to go with you!"

Abe interrupted and said, "Will, we put these things together for you; hopefully it is pretty much everything you'll need. I want you to take my extra mount too. She'll make the trip easier for you. Elizabeth and I are sick over this, and we won't stop praying."

Will was almost at a loss for words, but he swallowed the lump in his throat and said, "You two are true friends. Thanks for all of this."

Abe pulled some money from the top pocket of his shirt and handed it to Will.

"Money?" Will said in surprise.

"Yes; you'll need it! It's from all of us that care."

Will stuck the money in his pocket. With Loretta still in his arms, he gave her one last hug and a kiss before putting her down. "Loretta, I love you, and I'll be back soon with Mommy."

"Now get! And bring Emma back! Loretta will be fine here with us," Abe said.

Will mounted his horse and said, "Thanks again." As he rode off, he took one last look over his shoulder and saw his little girl waving goodbye.

Will hoped to find some kind of lead before he headed out. The two men may have left something behind. *They are human, a mistake is possible*, he thought.

Will was having a difficult time staying focused with the memories that were flooding his mind—Emma when they first met, their wedding day, the day Loretta was born. Similar to the slats on a picket fence when you ride by in a hurry, his memories were flying by in his mind.

His mind snapped back to the present situation and the black shadow of uncertainty that lay before him. *Is Emma alive? What kind of men am I pursuing?* he thought. Then Will cried out, "Lord, what did she or I do to deserve this?"

Once at his place Will sat in the saddle as if in a trance. *Get off your horse and go into the house,* he heard echo through his mind. Will jumped off and walked in through the front door. Once inside he realized that finding the needed evidence was not going to be an easy thing. Peterson and the other men had roamed through the house, adding their tracks to the kidnappers.

When he entered the bedroom, he found it as Peterson had said. The bed had been moved, and some things on the floor were broken. The dresser drawers were pulled out with most of the contents dumped on the bed. The bedroom looked like the rest of the house, upside down. The men were definitely looking for something, but what?

Will stood at the foot of the bed trying to imagine what Emma had gone through—her fears and cry for help—but there was no caring ones to hear before a strong hand covered her mouth and stopped the pleading. These thoughts made his heart sick. How could some people be so hard-hearted, especially to people who are so kind-hearted, people similar to Emma?

He found himself on his knees, praying like never before. With tears running down his face, he cried out, "Lord, help me! I'm filled with anger and insecurity. In a moment of time, I've lost Emma, maybe forever! I want to take revenge on these men; I want to kill them for what they've done to her. The pain in my heart, Lord, is almost too much to bear. The old man in me is so strong, and my faith is so weak. I don't know if I can stay faithful to You; I just don't know! This may be my undoing, Lord! Help me! Lord Jesus, what if I lose track of them? Please give me the wisdom to find her. I know so well that I'm a sinner, but I don't want to be! Please forgive me and give me the strength to bear this, and Lord, I ask You for peace. Father, in Jesus' name, I ask this. Amen."

As Will rose from his knees and turned to leave the room, he spotted Emma's Bible in the corner partly covered with some of the clothes that had been pulled from one of the dresser drawers. He bent over and picked it up, quickly thumbing through a few pages as he walked out of the room.

He noticed Emma's bonnet on one of the pegs by the back door. As he reached for the bonnet, it slipped from his fingers and floated to the floor. He squatted down to pick it up and then pulled it to his nose. The smell of her perfume lingered in the air, and he thought about how her long brown hair fell midway down her back.

In spite of Will's reminiscing, he noticed a few marks on the floor that he had never seen before. He moved closer for a more detailed look. Upon examination he knew he was looking at spur marks and a number of them. *Lord, thank you for this! One of the men drags a spur! It's possible that one of them has a bad hip or knee?* he figured.

Once outside the back door he found a few clear tracks, but most of them were muddled. He followed them a short distance to the creek. Deputy Peterson had been correct. They had gone up the creek, and there was nothing unusual about the tracks at the creek's edge. The horses were all shoed, and it didn't appear that either of the men were heavy or carrying a load. Everything was planned for speed.

I have so little time, Lord, he silently prayed. *Do I follow the creek or the main road? Which way would be the most productive? I've got to find Emma before it's too late. I don't know what else to ask, Lord. Please help me!*

As he reached Bella and climbed into the saddle, he felt impressed to head north on the main road. He now had his direction. A portion of his stress floated away like steam that is set free from a boiling pot when the pressure lifts its lid. He knew that finding Emma was going to be more a matter of faith than tracking skills. The roads in the area were widely used, and tracks didn't last long. The rain was another factor, making the tracks difficult to read. These factors were combined with the fact that his tracking skills weren't as good as he wished they were. No, he couldn't rely on tracking; he needed to focus on his faith in God.

He needed another man, a good man, to ride with him, because two are better then one. Going it alone was an unwise decision; death could arrive at any unexpected moment for him and the man who might ride with him.

He truly loved Emma, and if asked, he would die to save her. But he had to trust God and not in himself, so he rode north in search of his wife.

Chapter Two

The Lack of Unity

"If you guys would pick up the pace, we could make better time! We've got a long way to go before nightfall. And I don't want to hear from you, Charlie, that we should have kept the buckboard, that it would have made life easier if we did, for you know good and well that it was too slow," Lester forcefully barked. "It worked for our little plan of getting out of town unsuspected, but we need to travel faster now."

Charlie just grumbled under his breath and made no comment. He and Joey picked up the pace and closed the gap between Lester and them.

Emma also dared not say a word. She tried not to pay any attention to them. They had caused her enough pain and had scared her almost to death. Her treatment had been, and still was, a strange mixture of kindness and attacks meant to intimidate her.

Her emotions and mind were always on edge. She didn't have a mirror to look in, but she still knew her face and eyes were swollen from the almost continual crying. Also she had a headache that had started almost immediately after being kidnapped. The constant pounding added to her fatigue. She feared for her own well-being, though most of her focus was on Loretta and Will.

Would they be left alone, without a mother or wife?

She longed to see Loretta—to sit her once again on her lap and brush her light brown hair, to hold her little girl who was five and growing quickly. Emma could picture her in her light blue dress trimmed in white with her matching bonnet. Sometimes they would sit on the front porch and play dolls in the warm sun. Her mind wandered to the time they made an apple pie and Loretta had more apples on the floor and herself than in the pie tin, but what fun they had had learning to make that pie.

She remembered her last hug and kiss from Will before he rode out to interview for the new marshall's job. He was the love of her life. The scent of his aftershave and his gray-blue eyes, which sparkled when he smiled and sometimes when he laughed, always charmed her. When she became worried, he would hold her—his love and strength always comforted her.

They stole her away for a reason that was not obvious on the surface. In her mind's eye she could see the men as they searched through everything in the short time they had given themselves for the job. She couldn't make the connection to what they were looking for. *What do we have that they want?* she continued to ponder, but to no avail. She retraced the events of how they had threatened her with the words "Do as you're told and keep your mouth shut if you want to see tomorrow." Then they had shot a bullet into the ground for effect, nearly causing her to jump out of her skin. Lester had added an additional threat by pointing his gun at her head when she hesitated to climb into the coffin from fear of never climbing out.

The coffin was Lester's brainstorm. He believed it would make it easier to escape, posing as a simple man transporting his dear sister who had just passed away. It was a successful scheme, for no one thought otherwise. As a matter of fact, some passersby offered their condolences for his loss.

Emma's attention was jolted back to the present when she heard them bickering again. The dissension between the men only made the situation worse. They were clearly not at peace, and they did not seem united in this crime. *What kind of men are they?* she thought.

Lester was a tall man of medium build with deep-set brown eyes. He was angry and impatient and rarely smiled. He was the boss, and he liked it that way. Now Charlie Woodman, he was a man-pleaser, the nervous type, insecure, and at times it seemed as if he disliked himself very much. He was troubled

and haunted by a number of poor decisions along the way. He stood about 5'7"
and was stocky. Most of his thick black hair had disappeared years ago.

Surprisingly, Joey, the youngest of the three, was cut from a different piece
of cloth. He was slow-minded but had the strength of two men. Joey's love for
horses was strong; he understood them and could put them at peace. Being
slow made him withdraw at times—socializing could be exacting for him, so
keeping to himself just made his life easier. His kind side could be seen when
compared to the hard hearts of the two older men. He had helped Emma out a
few times, making a few moments more bearable for her.

Her thoughts migrated back to their previous position; she had no idea
where they were taking her. But she believed God knew; He and His angels
were always by her side. From the moment the men had entered her house, she
witnessed God's protective hand on her. The men hadn't beaten her or touched
her in any improper way. She was thankful for that, and she was alive.

She had never seen these men before until the day they carried her off. Her
many questions were almost endless, but they weren't saying a thing. There
was an air of secrecy to their plans, and they wanted to keep it that way. It was
clear that they wanted nothing to interfere with their plans. They talked a lot
but said very little. It reminded her of having a lot of thunder but not much
rain.

Lester gave Emma's reins a jerk, making the horse she rode leap forward,
something she disliked very much, especially when her hands were tied to
the horn of the saddle. She looked behind and to the right at Charlie and Joey
who were no longer lagging behind. She could see that Charlie looked very
uncomfortable; he was sweating profusely, not only did his shirt bear witness
to the fact but his hat was wet above the old sweat marks. He held something
against horses, which he kept to himself. One would think that he would have
chosen a different profession than one that required him to be in the saddle all
day long, but this job had him riding whether he liked it or not.

Suddenly Charlie piped up, "Lester! I'm getting off this horse. I'm sitting
down under this pine tree." He and Joey stopped their horses, climbed down,
and took their places in the shade.

Lester just rolled his eyes and said, "OK, Charlie, sit in the shade for a few
minutes." He knew he couldn't win this one since they had already dismounted.
"Come on, woman, let's sit in the shade." The words sounded sweet to Emma

because she needed a break from the ride, too.

She found a soft bed of pine needles to lie down on, and her whole being felt as if it could melt into the earth. She was feeling the effects of the ordeal—the stress, poor sleep, and the long days in the saddle. She wished she had her bonnet, for when the noonday sun was high above her head, it felt as if she was in a oven. But the men paid little attention to her needs. She took a few deep breaths and tried to relax in the moments given her.

Joey spoke up and asked, "How much more to go to do what you want to do, Lester?"

"Why it's simple, Joey. We're going to take the woman up north and sell her to the Indians or to an old lonely hermit; then we're done," Charlie said with a snicker.

That seemed to annoy Joey. He reached for Charlie as he said with half-clenched teeth, "No! You're not doin' that to her."

Lester hollered, "Stop, don't hurt him, Joey! Charlie's joking."

Joey stopped, but not before his powerful right hand took hold of Charlie's shirt and pulled him closer, nearly nose to nose. The expression on Charlie's face showed that he knew he had gone too far with his sarcasm. Joey let go of him, but not without saying, "You know I can hurt him real bad if I want to. Now, Lester, you tell him to stop it."

"I will, Joey! I promise," Lester said hurriedly. He continued on, "Let me assure you, Joey, we're not selling the woman or giving her away to anybody. Trust me! We've got better plans for her than that. We have much better plans for her than that!"

Was there any truth mixed in with the jokes, and what was the better plan? Emma's tears flowed once again down the sides of her unwashed face. She closed her eyes as her body began to shake from the stress of the twisted situation she found herself thrust into. As she thought it through, she knew Lester was telling the truth. She wasn't for sale; she was far more valuable than that. They had gone to great lengths, and it was too well planned. They wanted something from her; something they were willing to risk their lives for.

Lord, I ask You again; am I to live or die at their hands? What is going to be gained from this, Father? Is this my own doing? Have I turned someone against me? Please forgive me if I have, she silently pleaded. *Please, Lord! Please! I don't understand. If it is my fault, show me what I've done wrong.*

Father, please keep me safe like You did Joseph in Egypt. She continued to pray. *Please lead Will to me so he can take me home to my little girl, and Lord, help him and protect him. I thank you, Father, and I ask this in Jesus' name. Amen.*

When she had finished, she opened her eyes and realized that no one had moved or said a word as if time had stood still for a moment. The God of heaven had quieted her storm for the moment. He had answered her. Now she must wait for His will to be revealed.

Charlie stood up slowly and started to beat some of the trail dust off his clothes with his old weathered hat. It filled the air around him with a fine cloud of brown dust that had a strange odor and taste to it. It also made him cough and spit, which forced him to reach for his only canteen and take a long drink. Lester coughed and, pointing to a spot away from the group, said, "Thanks, Charlie, you could have walked over there to do that."

Soon after this episode, Lester jumped to his feet and gave the order, "Let's mount up! We still have the light to ride." He handed Charlie the reins to Emma's horse and said, "Don't lose her; she's too important!" Lester climbed into the saddle and waited for them with annoyance.

"Just relax, Lester! Where's the woman goin'? Do you expect her to ride off into the sunset for home? And talking about riding, we're headed to the territory, aren't we? That's our goal, the far north, isn't it? I can understand the hurry and not stopping at Marysville like we planned, but I need more information, more details about all of this." Charlie said this with a newfound confidence and strength as if he had just dug up the long sleeping young man of his youth.

Lester knew it was time to answer some questions. Joey was to know very little and the woman nothing at all. After they had ridden a distance, he signaled for Charlie to ride up closer. Charlie handed Emma's reins to Joey and rode up to Lester.

"Now, tell me the truth, my friend, about this job of ours," Charlie said as soon as he was beside Lester.

"I have," Lester said, "but there's more to it. I'm not the boss. We've been hired by Peter Wyler; he's the one who wants the woman."

Charlie was surprised to hear that, seeing that Lester acted as if all this was his doing. "So why all the mystery; I need reasons."

"He didn't give me any when we met, which was only twice. He told me what he wanted and what he'd pay. Wyler gave no reason for why he wanted the woman. That's it; he said very little. I think she means something to him, Charlie, because he strongly demanded, 'Don't hurt her or touch her in any way.' The woman and him have a connection to the past somehow. She has real value to him. What that value is I just don't know as of yet."

"Lester, you and I both know her pockets aren't full of money. Her man's only the sheriff. What does Wyler expect to get out of them? We tore the place apart and found nothing. Wait a minute! You knew what we were looking for, didn't you! My sly old fox of a friend. How stupid could I be; I just followed orders like a good soldier and asked very little."

"Charlie, that's why I've hired you for the last two jobs. You do a good job, and you don't ask any questions; you're safe. You know if you don't ask questions you don't have answers. You can't have an accidental slip of the tongue."

"Ya! You're right, Lester, but this job is different! It's not like the other jobs where we were just robbing and the like. This one makes us kidnappers; we could hang for this!"

"We could, but we won't. This job is too well thought out for things to go wrong."

"What were we looking for then? A map to a gold mine or something?"

"We were looking for anything that had value that we could line our own pockets with and no one else's," said Lester.

Charlie caught Lester's eye with a look of disbelief. "But we found nothing, just a broken watch—no guns and not a cent. We left with a woman and empty pockets," Charlie challenged.

"Well, Charlie, if we deliver her as ordered, we can ride away with a thousand each. That's not a bad paying job you know! And you said you wanted answers! I think when Wyler sees her we'll both get all the answers we want. Now remember, you gotta keep your mouth shut, especially around Joey. Next time I may not be able to stop him from hurting you, or worse, killing you."

"I hear ya, Lester!"

"Then stop harassing him. I don't want to shoot him just because you can't control that tongue of yours. Do you understand? We have a job to finish!"

Charlie nodded his head and said, "Yes, I understand. But Lester, can't you see that Joey favors the woman and sticks up for her?"

"Yes, I do, but you don't get it, do you, Charlie? Joey's our check and balance so that we don't hurt the woman and mess up the job. There's been a couple of times I could of slapped her around, especially when she wouldn't get into the coffin when I told her to, and there may be a few more times," Lester said with an obvious annoyance to his voice.

A small pine tree had fallen across the road. As they maneuvered around it, Emma spoke up, "Would you please let Joey untie my hands, Lester? The rope really hurts. I won't cause you any trouble, I promise, please?"

"Joey, go ahead! I'll just tie her up at night," Lester remarked.

Chapter Three

An Unexpected Answer

The sky was a soft gray with a few remaining patches of black clouds hovering overhead. The sun was making its appearance in striking shafts of white light. With the threat of rain lessening, Will felt relieved. He wasn't looking forward to another period of rain, since he lived almost entirely on the road these days. He wondered if Emma had to be exposed to the weather. He hoped and prayed that the men who had her would have enough brains to keep themselves and her out of the rain.

Marysville, a thriving city of about ten thousand people, was prosperous because of the gold around it. People came by droves to dig for its riches, which filled Marysville's banks with gold and gold dust to be sent to the U.S. mint in San Francisco. Since Marysville was situated on the banks of the Feather River, it was easy for the merchants to access the city. With all of this business, Marysville was able to support its many schools, churches, mills, factories, storefronts, and two daily newspapers. Marysville was proud of its brick buildings.

It was here that Will hoped to find a lead, some information that could point him to his sweetheart. With all of the eyes and ears that were moving to and fro each day, he was hopeful that something would spring up.

Will rode up to the mercantile store on Main Street, dismounted, and tied up his horse. He noticed a Chinese man standing in front of the store window. The man was looking inside as if he wanted something but couldn't have it. He was taller than the average Chinese person, and he stood straight like a soldier. Will grabbed his rifle and saddle bag as the Chinese man moved away from the window and headed down the boardwalk.

At the same time two men stepped out of the saloon in the direction of the Chinese man. The three of them met on the boardwalk with one of the two men saying, "Hey! Look at this, old buddy. What do we have here? Why it looks like a John to me, wouldn't you say so…"

"Yep, he sure does," the older man replied to the younger man. "And look! He's dressed like us; maybe he don't want to be Chinese anymore, and his hair's all grown out, too. I'd say he wants to be just like us!"

The Chinese man tried to pass, but the older one stepped in his way. "I'm talkin' to you, Chinaman. Don't walk away from me when I'm talkin' to you!"

The Chinese man stood still and listened to the words of abuse as if it was an evil thing to be Chinese, as if he should live in shame because of it.

The older one spoke again with a tone in his voice that showed annoyance with the man for saying nothing. "Can't you talk, John? Did someone snatch your tongue? Say something, Chinamen. Say something!"

Will listened in the background with the small crowd that had started to gather. Will stepped up on the boardwalk and pressed through a few people. He had heard all he cared to. He said with the authority of the lawman that he was "You guys have had too much to drink, and you've had your fun with him and then some, so be on your way!" The three of them, along with some in the crowd, looked on in surprise.

The older man, who Will had heard been called Old Buddy, moved toward him. Looking up at Will with his head cocked to the left, he sneered, "Just who might you be to be telling us what to do? Are you some kind of a protector of this John, well are ya?"

The aggressive man in Will came rushing to the forefront. Will wanted to take their guns and lock them up, but he knew this wasn't his town. At that moment the Lord spoke in a quiet voice that only He can do when it's needed most: "Blessed are the peacemakers." This redirected Will's thoughts.

Will looked the man in the eye and said in a serious voice, "I'm not here to fight with you two, but don't you think that this Chinese man has the same right to live here in peace just like you do?"

For a moment the man was caught off guard. He then said in a rushed manner, "Come on, Art, let's go! If this guy wants the John, he can have him— if he loves him that much." The two men pushed their way through the crowd and disappeared.

Will and the Chinese man stood there looking at each other as the crowd started to break up. The Chinese man spoke first, "Thank you for helping me out, but why? Nobody helps the Chinese but the Chinese."

Will was surprised by his excellent English. He just smiled and said, "I'm Will Jacobs, and I don't see it that way." Will offered his hand in friendship, so the Chinese man reached out and took it.

"I'm Yann Chang; I just came up from San Francisco."

"Well, Yann, I'm from Stone Ridge, and I'm heading north. It's nice to meet you; take care."

The marshall's office was the first stop in hopes of some news that would lighten his heart. The sign on the door read Marshall Frank Owens. The marshall was standing next to the filing cabinet with the drawer open. He turned and asked "What can I do for you?" as the door shut.

"Marshall Owens?" Will asked.

"Yes, I'm he," the marshall replied.

"I'm Will Jacobs, the sheriff of Stone Ridge."

"It's good to meet you, Jacobs." The marshall had moved to his desk and was now sitting on one of its corners. "What brings you up this way, sheriff?" he asked.

"I need some information; some solid leads. I'm searching for my wife and the two men who kidnapped her."

"Your wife's been kidnapped!" Owens said with raised eyebrows.

"Yes, from our place while I was out of town. I followed their tracks, but I lost them north of Stone Ridge; I'm guessing they headed this way. Have you or your deputies seen two men and my wife riding through, and in a hurry, I'm sure." He continued, "My wife is five-six, good looking, with long brown hair, which she wears down most of the time. All I know about the two men is that one of them drags a spur—there's something wrong with the way the man walks."

"I think the men passed us by. I have four deputies, and they've said nothing about this nor reported seeing anything suspicious. Neither have I. I'm sorry about your wife, Jacobs. I wish I had them locked up and your wife over at the inn waiting for you. I'd hate to lose my wife that way. Do you have any children?" Owens asked.

"Yes, one girl, five years old," Will answered.

"There's a trading post north of here about fifteen miles. They get a lot of passersby. Maybe they would have a lead for you."

Will was deeply disappointed. "No one has seen a thing at Johnson Ranch, Nicolaus, or even the ferry? These guys are good. I'm riding alone, and they have a two-day start on me. Maybe I missed something along the way."

"You could hire a tracker, but I have no men to spare, Jacobs," Owens commented.

"A tracker! I don't have that kind of cash!" Will said with that familiar knot in his stomach. "This could take months. May God help me find her."

"I've never had much use for religion, but to each his own," Owens said indifferently.

"Thanks for your time and for trying to help," Will said.

"Sorry I couldn't do more for you. Oh, by the way, Jacobs, you did a good job taking care of Muller. The word came up this way that the sheriff of Stone Ridge killed him in a gunfight. It's nice to meet the man that stopped him. He spent a little time here before he ended up your way. I had to lock him up for a night because he had too much whiskey for any one man," Owens said.

"It wasn't fun," commented Will.

"It never is. We have a tough job, us lawmen. We take the job in hopes of making the town a better place to live for our families and others, but the downside is that at times we have to kill so others can live. I understand your feelings. But let me add this, don't be discouraged about not finding the leads right off. They will show up; I know from experience that they will," replied Owens.

"Thanks for the encouragement," said Will as he closed the door behind him.

૭ಿ૭ಿ૭ಿ૭ಿ૭ಿ

As Will walked out of the dry goods store with a number of fresh supplies,

25

he spotted Yann standing by the hitching post holding the reins to his mount. He seemed to be a mystery just waiting to be solved. "Yann, what do you need?" Will asked.

"I need to ride with you."

"Why is that, Yann?"

"You helped me when you didn't have to. I feel I can trust you, and maybe you can use my help, if you agree," Yann said with a straight face.

"Can you track? I need an extra pair of eyes," Will asked.

"Yes, in China I tracked many things, but I have never been north of here," Yann answered.

"Well, I've only been north of here once myself, and you might be right; it may turn out that we can help each other. So let's head out."

As they rode out of Marysville, they were both lost in their own thoughts. Will was struggling with his trust in God's providence—his faith was weak; the fear had returned, and now his mind was overcome with doubt. Would he find Emma alive, or worst yet, would he ever find her at all? If he did find her, would the two men stop him and kill him first?

His state of mind forbade him from thinking clearly and reasoning his way through his fears. Then the thought came to him, *What if your worst nightmare came true? What would you do? Would you give up, throw away your faith? There is Loretta; what type of father would you be then? Would you still serve the Lord like Job did? He suffered so much loss.* Those words struck Will's heart like a blacksmith's hammer striking a piece of steel.

He understood that a humble and obedient heart was well pleasing to the Lord and would open the door to the blessings of God. As they rode in silence, Will prayed, *Lord, You have read my thoughts, and You have the solution to all of this. Forgive me for my lack of faith and trust in You. I'm fearful of what's coming, Lord. I need Your strength and confidence in Your promises. Make me just like You, Jesus. You told me to be strong and of good courage and not to be afraid nor dismayed because You are with me wherever I go. Make me strong in You, Lord, in Your name, amen.*

Yann spoke up and said, "Will, I have many questions to ask you."

"What do you want to know?"

"Who are you, and who are we tracking?"

"I'm the sheriff of Stone Ridge. I'm tracking two men who kidnapped my wife, but I know very little about them. One of the men drags a spur; I think maybe it's a bad leg. They rode north, but I know little else about them. My wife's name is Emma, and we have a five-year-old little girl named Loretta. She's being taken care of by good friends back home."

He paused, took a breath, and then continued. "You may be thinking that if I'm the sheriff how could my wife be kidnapped? Well, I was gone for four days, traveling east of home looking at a marshall's job, when it happened. I thought a better job with an increase in pay would be a great opportunity for us. Emma asked me not to take the job because she loves the town we are in and is happy there. As a man I had to try to improve our situation. At least I thought so, but now I see I was wrong. This wouldn't have happened if I hadn't gone on the job interview."

"That may not be true, Will. If they were going to take her, they still could have. All you had to do was leave your house for the day; that's all," Yann commented.

"That question eats at me often. I'll just have to wait and see how it all works out when I learn the reason for her kidnapping. Emma's a good woman, and I don't want to live without her. She and I have a strong love for each other. I liked her the first time I saw her, and I'm not the same man without her. May God help us," Will said with a sigh.

"At least you have a wife to go and search for and a daughter to leave behind. I have nether. I may never have Sanne, the one I love, as my wife. I left all behind and ran for my life," Yann said.

"So ... you are running from someone? They must be powerful to make you run all the way from China and to keep you running. When I first saw you looking in the store window, you looked mysterious. So you didn't come to California to dig for gold but to hide," Will stated, half knowing the answer.

"Yes, I was forced to leave China. I would have been executed if I stayed. I'm accused of being part of a plan to kill the governor. I was the governor's personal bodyguard, which included his wife and children. There were five other guards, and we all worked together. I trained most of my life to have the honor of that position."

"So, what went wrong, Yann?"

"I wanted a night off, and it was my responsibility to find someone to fill in for me, and that I did. That's the night they tried to kill the governor and his family. They weren't successful, but they did kill the guard who took my place. Something or someone stopped them, and the family was unharmed.

"Since I was having dinner with Sanne and her family and not guarding the governor, they concluded that I must be part of the plan to destroy the governor and his family. I was warned that they were after me. My father's friends helped me escape by ship that same night. My father gave me some money, which has made things easier. I've only been here for four months, but long enough to know I'm not free from the grip of the governor.

"Two men were sent to bring me back to China. They found me in San Francisco. One of the men was in school with me, though we were never friends. I think he must have volunteered for the job. But his training was inferior. He tried to stop me as I came out of my rented room. He met me in the hallway and told me why he had come. I told Mui not to stand in my way, but he would not hear me, so I fought him and escaped."

"Yann, did you kill him?" Will asked.

"No, I didn't. I just hurt him a little. Mui is not the problem. It's the second man. I went to get my horse and had just mounted to ride when he came out of nowhere and took hold of my reins. He said, 'Yann, you can't run or hide. I'm very patient; I'm taking you back to China.' Then he let go of my reins. He said it with a smile and a strange kind of laugh. Then I rode away to Marysville.

"They will never give up; I know that. It would be shame and dishonor to them. They would rather die than go back to China empty-handed. So I have been given no other choice but to run."

Yann continued his story. "I worked hard. I was faithful to the governor. I honored him and brought honor to my family, but this is the end of it all— running for my life like a scared rabbit. I have left my life in China; Sanne is gentle, and to me, she is beautiful. She is intelligent, and she is also an artist. She works with her father who is a potter. He has made me part of his own family, and that also is an honor.

"Sanne and I wanted many children, but now, that's not possible. I am sick at heart, like you are, for what has been lost," Yann said sadly.

"What about the second man? Do you know him?"

"No, I don't; that's the problem!" Yann answered. "The man that hunts me is like a man from nowhere. He just shows up, and based on the way he moves, I know he is a master, but from where? I keep asking myself that again and again, but I find no answer to my question," Yann explained.

"Yann, for two men who are from different worlds, we are very much alike. The Lord has ways that are unknown to us. He always has the answer, and sometimes a surprise around the corner."

"You're a Christian," Yann said in a matter-of-fact way.

"Yes, Yann, I am. I believe Christ to be who He said He is: the Savior of the world, the Son of the living God. He has forgiven me for all my sins, and if I'm faithful, He will take me to heaven when He returns. He answers prayers and sends help. Look! He put us together when we needed help."

"I know parts of the Bible and about Christ. I was raised Buddhist until I was nine; then my Father became a Christian. He told us that he was wrong about Buddha and that he must teach us about Christ, who is the true God. My Father worked for the American Tea Company. It was there that he met Robert Bolton, a man from New York. He became very close to our family, and he came and taught us about Christ every week. As we studied the Bible, we were also taught to read and write in English. I have and still do surprise people with my fine English—it came easy to me at the age of nine.

"My father is very bright, and he wanted to know everything he could about the Bible. And as I just said, as my father studied, the whole family also studied along with Mr. Bolton. My older brother became very angry and rejected the idea of Christ being the one true God. He remained loyal to Buddha and has very little to do with our family any longer. My mother is a quiet and gentle woman; she has said very little about my father's faith, so I don't know if she really believes, but my young sister has a very strong faith, like my father."

"Where does this leave you? Do you believe?"

"I'm confused and troubled! That's where it leaves me. I want to believe; I want the happiness that my father and sister have, but I don't. That is the difficulty of being taught two different ways. It leaves me with the great question—which way do I turn, which road do I travel?"

"Are you open to learning more about Jesus Christ?" Will asked. "If He was to show you that He is the true God, would you then believe? I can tell you from my own personal experience that if you give the Lord half a chance He will more than prove Himself to you. Just be open to Him and see."

"I don't know. I'm confused; I just don't know," Yann sighed.

"Yann Chang! I'm going to ask the Lord to show you beyond a shadow of a doubt that He is the Lord who you can put your trust in."

"If it pleases you, go right ahead and do it. Like I said, I just don't know!"

"It would please me, Yann, to see you believe." Will didn't know what else to say, so he rode on.

The hard rains had given the landscape the fuel for a growth spurt. Wildflowers were in full bloom with the many different colors and shades that appeared, proving that summer had come. Will hadn't paid much attention lately, but it felt good to ride and relax a little bit. He remembered the trading post that should be coming into view soon if indeed it was the fifteen miles the marshall said it was, so he shared his thoughts with Yann. "The trading post should be just up ahead. Dusk is on its way, so I hope we are almost there."

"If the post is too far to reach before dark, we'll have to stop off the trail for the night. It looks like more rain is coming, so the post better be around the next bend. Since I was a child, I never liked getting my leathers wet," Yann said.

"I hope we don't get anymore rain. Just an hour ago it looked as if it was passing us by and we would stay dry. The horses don't need to get wet either for that matter. It's hard to tell what fifteen miles are like when all you have is unfamiliar landmarks. Maybe the marshall was off on his miles," Will commented.

"Will, there's something I've been thinking about for the past few minutes. How are you going to deal with the men when we catch up with them? What if they try to kill you or your wife? How do you reconcile that with your faith in Christ?" Confusion filled Yann's mind. He asked the questions more for himself than out of really wanting to know what Will's feelings were on the situation.

"Yann, I really don't know what I'm going to do. Sometimes I want to kill them for what they've done, then the next moment I feel like taking them back to stand trial so they can spend some time behind bars. That would give them plenty of time to think about their crime. All situations aren't the same. There are a few gray areas in this life. If they try to stop me from rescuing my wife, I hope the Lord will step in. He has a better plan than me shooting them.

"The Lord knows what's in my heart, and He knows how to make all thing work to the good. I have to trust Him," Will said.

"There's the trading post!" Yann said, pointing up ahead.

"A bit more than fifteen miles wouldn't you say?"

The trading post sat off the road to the right on a small rise facing west. It was log built and longer than it was wide. Its builder had constructed a front porch that offered some shade to rest under. On the right side of the building they had extended the roof to add a mid-size stable that could house a dozen horses. Both ends were boxed in as a windbreak to protect the poor beasts from the weather.

They tied up their mounts and entered the front door near the stable. The lighting inside was poor. There were only two small windows in the building, but no lamps were lit. Will saw two doors—the one he had just walked through and one toward the middle left side of the building. The light that did shine in helped, but it still wasn't enough, and the left front corner of the building had nether window nor light—it was as dark as night. As Will's eyes slowly adjusted, he could see shelves to his left and right stocked, or partially stocked, with a variety of goods.

The building also offered a few tables and chairs. A counter ran most of its width with a number of different sized barrels sitting in front of it. A scale hung on a pole to the center left of the counter. There were also shelves that sat behind the counter that were divided by a door that led outside or to a back room, maybe living quarters.

Will caught sight of a cook stove on the far left side of the counter by the side door. There was no one in sight. As Will stepped up to the counter, he turned to Yann and said, "Do you see anybody?" Just then the door in front of them opened, and a woman stepped out.

"I thought I heard someone. What can I do for you men?"

Will smiled and said, "Miss, we need a few things, such as grain for our horses and a hot meal so we don't have to cook ourselves, and some information!"

"Grab a chair and sit down, and I'll feed you. All I have is biscuits and gravy with corn and beans."

"That will do fine!" Will said with relief, and they sat down at a small table across from each other.

Yann set his hat on the table and looked at Will as he said, "We need a plan, more to go on. We're just riding to nowhere."

"It may appear that way, but we're going in the right direction. I know we are. I can feel it right here," he said as he put his hand to his chest and patted it twice. The woman appeared with two plates of hot food and set them down along with their forks. She stepped back a few feet from the table and placed both hands in the pockets of her apron. As they started to eat, she stood there and looked them over with a very discerning eye.

"You two are an unlikely pair, I'd say. You're not the typical kind I see in here. That's not wrong, mind you, but there's something here I don't get, and I'm gonna work on it until I figure things out." Turning on her heels, she headed back to her cook stove.

Yann looked up from his plate and said, "She's right, a Chinese and white man traveling together in this land. It's unheard of, and it could be dangerous for one or both of us." Will nodded his head in agreement as he shoved another bite of beans and corn into his mouth. "I'll go and grain the horses after I finish eating," Yann stated.

After Yann left for the stable, Will stared at the chair that was now empty in front of him as he finished off his plate of food. The sound of a metal spoon hitting the top of the cook stove grabbed his attention. He turned his head to see the woman pick up the spoon from the floor and then place it on the countertop. She then reached into a jar and said out loud, "I've got it!!" She quickly moved toward his table. "You're Will, aren't you?"

Will felt his body jerk from shock, and his eyes grew huge. He pushed his chair back and stood up, and with a voice full of emotion, he said, "They've been here! Emma's been here!"

"Yes," she said. "I was trying to remember how Emma described you, and it finally clicked. By the way, I'm Marie Rose, and I have this for you." She handed Will a seashell that she pulled from the pocket of her apron.

Will held the shell for a moment and stared at it. His mind raced back to that day in San Francisco, the day he had found this little shell in the sand on the beach. That same afternoon he had walked into a clothing store to buy a new hat and there stood Emma, smiling and saying "Do you need any help? If you do, I'll be glad to assist you." Will had been on a short vacation and was leaving the next day to return to Stone Ridge where he was to start as their new deputy. After taking his time buying his new hat, he had asked her to dinner for that very night, and he had given her the seashell as a keepsake.

"Are you all right?" Marie Rose asked.

"Yes, yes, I am. Finish what you were telling me about the shell."

"Well, when she handed it to me, she said, 'Give this to Will when he comes, and tell him I love him.' She said it with tears in her eyes, but she said it with confidence. She knew you would come! Those men kidnapped your wife, didn't they?"

"Yes, they did! How did she look?"

"She looked worn out, unkempt, and afraid. When she put the shell in my hand, she did it quick, and then she moved away from the counter. The two men that came in with her watched her closely. She did well to hand me the shell and say a few words," Marie Rose said.

"Only two men were with her, right?"

"No! There were three men; the third stayed outside with the horses. They all ate outside, and no one said much at all. Then they rode off."

"I've been tracking two men. That's all I thought there were. What did the men look like? Can you remember? I need to know; it's very important!" Will said with urgency in his voice.

"Well, one was tall and kind of medium built with dark eyes—he could look right through you. The second man I can't forget. He was shorter, stocky, and almost bald; the little hair he had was black. What caught my eye the most was his peculiar walk. He dragged his right foot a little bit which made the spur jingle more than the other."

"Tell me about the third man," Will said.

"The third was just about the same height as the second, but he was strong, really strong, and it seemed like he'd rather be with the horses than with people. He smiled and was courteous," she said.

"Did my wife look like she had been beaten or anything?"

"Not that I could see. She'd been crying though; her face and eyes were puffy. I also remember her wrists. They looked red and swollen, like she had been tied up."

All of this was like a two-edged sword, giving Will new hope, and more pain. Emma was alive and in fair condition. That gave him great hope. He was thankful for this answered prayer.

"Now, Marie Rose, how many days ago were they here?" Will asked, almost holding his breath.

"Three days ago."

"Three days ago! They've gained a day on me. I must've missed something."

"Not necessarily; it's easier to run than it is to track!" came a voice from the lightless corner that Will's eyes could hardly penetrate.

"That may be true. But since I don't know you, why don't you show yourself," Will stated.

A tall man stood up, stepped out into the light, and walked up to Will. A large dog that resembled a wolf followed him. The dog growled, showing a healthy set of teeth and making it known that this was his world and no one dared intrude into it. The man spoke to the dog, "Max, it's all right. Lie down!" He put out his oversized hand to shake Will's hand as he introduced himself. "My name is Tanger, and I've been listening to what's been said. It makes my blood hot just hearing it. I live in the territory, and I know it well. It would give me real satisfaction to help you track them down."

"Tanger, I'm Will Jacobs, the sheriff of Stone Ridge down south. Thanks for offering, but I can't pay you, neither can I promise that you won't get shot. I don't know what I'm heading into."

"I'm not asking to be paid, Jacobs! I said it would give me real satisfaction to track them down. Men that steal other men's wives irritate me! You think it over, and let me know. I'm leaving in the morning for the territory."

"I don't need to think it over. I'd like to take you up on the offer."

"Good! I was hoping you'd see it my way," said Tanger.

"But I'm leaving now, not in the morning! I have to find my wife. She's out there somewhere, and now they have three days lead on me."

"Jacobs, we can't ride now! It's starting to rain, and the sun has gone down. Riding through the night won't get us any farther ahead, and it would be good for us to stay and sleep. It's warm and dry here."

"The horses are grained and bedded down for the night, and I brought the gear in," explained Yann. Will hadn't noticed him come back in with all the excitement.

"Sit down and let's talk awhile," suggested Tanger.

Marie Rose interrupted, "You've got yourself one fine man. He knows the territory better than most men, and he's a great tracker. Why, look at his size! He's six foot four."

"Marie Rose! Stop bragging on me!" Tanger said quickly.

"No! I won't stop! He's got to know that you're a great shot with that rifle, and you have an eye like an eagle. And you mean what you say—you keep your word. I don't know a man tougher than you! I'm finished. Now I'll leave you men to talk."

As she walked away, Will said, "It looks like she favors you, Tanger."

"Marie Rose is married to Edger Newly. They own and run this place together. He's in Marysville doin' some business; he'll probably be back tomorrow. I met them when Half Moon introduced us back in '48. She favors me like a brother," Tanger said.

"Well, I guess I'm wrong about her," Will said as he moved in his chair. "Who's Half Moon? You've pricked my curiosity," Will said.

"He's a mountain man who gave up trapping in the mid-30s and now lives in the territory. I met him about a month after my mother and I got here. He helped me become the man I am, and he's like a father to me. He helped with the lose."

"So, you're father's dead?" Will asked.

"Yeah, he died of the fever. He was a good man; I miss him still. My mother caught the fever, too, but she pulled through it. She's never regained all her strength back though. But that's enough of digging up old memories," Tanger said.

A crack of lightning grabbed their attention, reminding Will that Yann had been right, a bad storm had moved in. He hoped it would clear by morning. If not, the busy wagon road would be a mess of mud, puddles of water, and maybe a few downed trees.

Turning to Yann, Tanger said, "I don't think we've been introduced yet. What's your name?"

"My name is Yann Chang," the Chinese man replied.

"How do you fit into all of this? Are you from Stone Ridge too?"

"No, Will helped me out of trouble in Marysville, so I asked to ride with him."

"It's amazing the way things work," Will said. "I started out chasing two men alone, and now the three of us are chasing three. I'd say the odds are in our favor now. The Lord has ways of taking care of the messes that men get themselves into."

35

"I don't know if God took care of this or not," Tanger replied. "I was here, and I heard everything. I offered to help you out because of your situation. That's it."

Will had the feeling that Tanger was short on patience when it came to religious things, so he let the subject drop. "Well, I'm going to get some sleep. I think I'll just lay my bedroll down by the stove if that's OK," Will stated.

As Will moved toward the stove, he remembered the dog. "Tanger, will your dog bother me in the night?"

"Max, come here!" The dog immediately got up and came over. "Show him the back of your hand," Tanger said. Will offered Max his right hand for inspection. Max hesitated, so Tanger said, "It's all right, boy. Go ahead; he's a friend." The dog took a few steps forward and sniffed Will's hand twice, then he turned and walked back to where he had come from and lay back down.

With that settled, Will turned to his new traveling companions and said, "Let's leave early in the morning, so we can get a good start."

"Don't worry; we'll be ready to ride when you are!" Tanger said as he scratched his check through his thick reddish-brown beard.

Will was beat, and he needed sleep, but the thought that Emma had been there and was alive gave him much to think about and to be thankful for. The Lord was good. He had given Will more than he had asked for already. Will just had to keep holding on to his faith. As he lay on the wood floor and stared up at the ceiling, he whispered, "Jesus, forgive me again for doubting Your providence. You are all powerful, and You know everything. You amaze me how You do the things You do! Emma hasn't been out of Your sight for a moment, has she Lord! Thank you for the seashell, for leading me here, and for Tanger and Yann. Please bless Loretta, take care of her, Lord, till we get back. For all of this I thank you, and in Your name Jesus, I ask this, amen."

Will drifted off to sleep, not even realizing that Max was walking around his sleeping form, sniffing him as he went. Max had the habit of protecting his world and those he felt were a part of it. After walking around Will, Max lay down at Tanger's feet.

"You like the sheriff, don't you, boy?"

"Where do you think we should go from here, Tanger?" Yann asked.

"That's hard to say. We know she's alive, and they're headed north, but how far north, that's hard to figure. Are the men taking her to Oregon territory or are they staying here in California? There are mining camps, mountains, ravines, lakes, and a lot of heavy timberland for them to get lost in if they want to."

After a slight pause, Tanger voiced a question of his own. "Do you know why she was taken?"

"No, I don't, and Will doesn't either. She was kidnapped when he was out of town."

"I was thinking that if we knew why she was taken it may help us find her. What if these guys want Will to find them? Maybe they really want him and not his wife, or maybe the kidnappers want both of them. His wife is the honey that will catch the bee. Look at the lead that she left behind with the seashell and all. Were the men careless or did they drop a few clues along the way? It's a lot to think about," mused Tanger.

"Will told me that he and his wife don't hide anything from each other."

"Maybe that's the way it is now, but what about their lives before they met? We all have things we want to keep to ourselves."

"I'm not a mind reader, Tanger. And I don't know if this makes sense to me. I can't go on the assumption that they want us to find them. We could talk to Will about the possibility of a trap being set for him, but I guess we'll soon find out if that assumption is right or not," Yann replied.

"I've done a lot of tracking, but it's been mostly game with a few men mixed in. If a man doesn't want to be caught, he can be tough to hunt down because there's a lot of tricks he can use to allude you. I think they want Will to find them, the more I think about it," Tanger said.

"Right now, I can't see it clearly," Yann interjected.

"You'll see it; I can guarantee that," responded Tanger.

"I'd like to know what kind of trouble Will helped you out of, if you don't mind my asking."

"I don't have anything to hide," Yann said. "Here's my story. When I was in Marysville, two drunk guys were harassing me for dressing like an American and being Chinese. The situation looked like it was going to become violent, so Will stepped in and put a stop to it. He treated me as an equal, like a man, not as most treat the Chinese. They call us Johns and treat us like dogs.

"I arrived in San Francisco by ship four months ago. I was running for my life, hoping to find a little peace and safety, but I have found neither. In China they want to put me to death for a crime I didn't commit. I saw that Will and I could help each other, so I offered to ride with him. I can already tell that you also treat a man for who he is and not for what he looks like," Yann concluded.

"That I do. I've been treated well by a lot of people. It's the man and not his color that's important to me. But if someone does me harm when it's not called for, it takes me a long time to get over it. It kind of eats at me if you know what I mean."

"Yes, some things can be hard to get over. I'm being forced to run like a scared rabbit, but this rabbit didn't steal from his master's garden," Yann said with a bit of anger.

"Maybe we can take care of the men who are hunting you after we give Will a helping hand," Tanger commented.

"Of the two men who have come after me only one of them is a problem. He will be difficult to stop; that's why he's called a master. He is like a man from nowhere; he just shows up. When I think of him, a snake comes to mind. You don't know it's there until it bites you and injects its poison."

"We have harassment ahead of us and behind us. We could find ourselves in a real fix. I think a challenge is good for a man. It gives him a stronger character and sharpens his mind," Tanger said with a slight grin.

"The way Will's been snoring he's going to be up and ready to ride by sunrise. I should turn in too," Yann said.

Tanger nodded, then he stood up and headed for the back door with Max quickly following at his heels. When Tanger came back in, Yann was also dead to the world. He noticed that Yann was using his saddle to prop his head up like a pillow. *He's going to have some kind of a stiff neck in the morning,* he thought. He put out the lamp and turned in himself.

ॐॐॐॐॐ

The next morning Will was the first one up. Even before the sun was up, Will had eaten, saddled Bella and the extra mount, and was packed and ready to ride. He was just waiting on Yann and Tanger to get ready.

As Will waited, he sat on the porch with Emma's Bible. He thanked the Lord for the blessings he had received, many of which were beyond what he had imagined they could be. He gained strength from some of his favorite verses, and he sat in amazement as he contemplated the power of God to understand his thoughts. The Lord pointed him to Psalm 124, which led his heart to see how much he had doubted the love, care, and protection of the God of heaven. He turned to the front of the Bible where Emma had written down one of her poems.

He read it:

"You plucked me out of the fire, Lord, and placed me on higher ground.
Unworthy as I am, dear Lord, I know that Your grace abounds.
Create a greater miracle, make me just like Thee.
Save me from myself, dear Lord, please do Your will in me.
Plant me like an old oak tree."

The poem showed that her faith and depth of understanding were greater than his. He needed to grow and to see faith more clearly. He needed to fully embrace the fact that there was no aspect of his life that Christ was not involved with, even the hairs on his head were counted!

Will stood up and moved toward Bella, placing the Bible back in his saddlebag as Tanger and Yann joined him on the front porch. As Will mounted, Tanger said with a wide smile, "Are you ready?"

"Yes, sir. Let's go find my treasure," Will said, and they started to ride.

Chapter Four

A Short Delay

"I've been thinking, Tanger, about what you said over breakfast. It's possible and it makes some sense, but I can't get past the thought of Emma hiding something so important from me that she'd be kidnapped for it," said Will.

"I could be wrong, just like any other man, and maybe I am, but there's the clues that were left behind at the trading post. Would you say that the men were careless, maybe stupid? Could it be just dumb luck, or are they leading us into a trap? I'd like to think it was just dumb luck," Tanger responded.

"Emma doesn't hide things from me!" Will snapped.

"Will, try to get beyond that. Your wife had a life before she met you, and maybe she has some shame, something that's better left buried in the past. Tell me what man can say that he has a clean closet? I've never met one."

"No one; we've all failed. It's just hard for me to see her any other way except the way I do and that's being a good woman I'd die for. Tanger, you don't know what a fine wife she is—loving, faithful, and a wonderful mother to my little girl."

"I know it's hard for you to see it my way," Tanger replied. "And I hope

I'm wrong for both your sakes. I wish I had a wife to love and respect the way you do; maybe I will someday."

"If you did you'd understand my view better and why I defend her the way I do. But anyway, what more can you tell me about the Modoc?"

Before answering, Tanger watched a red shoulder hawk fly overhead just above the trees with that familiar cry *kee-aah-kee-aah*, as if it was saying see ya, see ya. It reminded him of that age old dream of man ... not to be earth bound but to fly free as a bird.

"Good question. The Modoc are fierce and warlike. They've been harassing and killing emigrants since '47; they do it mostly on the south trail. Last fall they killed sixty-five emigrants—men, women, and children. The incident was called Bloody Point. That happened just east of Tule Lake. If one wants to stay alive, it's best to steer clear of the Modoc.

"Now bear with me, and I'll tell you about the Klamath and two other tribes. The Klamath and the Modoc are bitter enemies; their hate for each other goes back a long ways. The Klamath have caused some trouble, but most of the time they're fairly peaceful people. The Paiutes is another tribe that's warlike; their warriors are fierce, and they have pushed down from the mountains northeast of here.

"The Pit River Indians, another tribe in these parts, are a peaceful people most of the time. They have great skill in basket making and hunting, and they're one of the largest tribes here. They live out their lives in terror because they live between the Paiute and the Modoc. Of the two, they fear the Modoc the most. The Modoc routinely raid the Pit River Tribe, killing their men and capturing the women and children, which helps the Modoc enlarge their own tribe.

"If the men we're after know their way around, they'll avoid taking the Nobles Trail east from Fort Reading that leads to the Applegate Trail. If they do take it, they could ride into a hornet's nest. Tule Lake and Lower Klamath Lake are off the Applegate. I've steered clear of it all since Bloody Point took place," Tanger explained.

"It doesn't sound hopeful."

"I'm not going to say they can't make it through; some have, but I hope they stick with the wagon road."

"I pray they have the good sense to," Will commented.

"Do you really believe in religion that much?" Tanger asked.

"Yes, I do. God has proven to me that He is real. He answers me when I pray. Just look at the seashell Emma left for me. He is leading," Will said.

"We have a good ride ahead of us before we reach Fort Reading, so there's plenty of time for this praying of yours to be done," Tanger said with a hint of sarcasm in his voice.

The three of them pulled off to the side of the road to let four supply wagons go by that were heading south. They had teams of four mules each, but the odd thing was that the wagons were empty. Not a good way to turn a profit. The wagons should be full of goods both ways.

Max came trotting over to Tanger as the wagons passed. He liked to run ahead, smelling, exploring, and sometimes scaring up a meal if possible. But he rarely let his master out of his sight. Tanger liked that quality about him. He wanted Max to stay independent and a little wild; he felt it made for a better dog.

The day wore on slowly but steadily with the flow of wagons and riders. Tanger and Will spoke to those who would be spoken to. Will felt sorrow for Yann who had to live in the shadows. He smiled little and spoke to few strangers, seeing the prejudice and hate of the people toward the Chinese. Sometimes it was hard to tell who the masses hated more: the Chinese or the Indians. It was clear that both nationalities had a difficult road ahead of them.

"We won't make Lassen's Ranch tonight, but we should be there by mid-morning tomorrow. I know it's not good news to you, Will, but if you remember, I told you that it's faster to run than it is to track," stated Tanger.

They rode on till dusk and then found a place to camp for the night. With the horses cared for and a fire built, it was time to rest. Tanger sat down on his horse blanket and leaned against his saddle. He opened his saddle bag and said, "I have a gift from Marie Rose for us."

"What would that be?" Yann and Will said almost in unison.

"Fresh bread and chicken, that's what! You know this would cost a lot of money in some places."

"Well, cheese and sardines with two or three slices of bread was thirty to thirty five dollars in Marysville," Yann stated.

"Gold. It's all because of gold and greed. Not all of us pan for it, and not everybody who does pan makes much. Some men walk away after a year of panning in debt because of the high cost of all the goods. It's not for me," Tanger said.

Max walked toward the fire and lay down next to Tanger who reached out and rubbed the dog's head. "Max, where you been?" he said as he stretched out his legs.

They all sat relaxing by the fire. Will finally broke the silence by asking, "Tanger, what's your first name? You must have one?"

"I have one all right, and I'd rather keep it to myself."

"I won't laugh or poke fun. Relax. I'm just curious."

"I haven't told anybody in years, and when it comes to mind, it just irritates me."

"Why's that?"

"Why's that! It's because of what happened."

"Do you hate your name, or the person that gave it to you?"

"Why do you need to know?"

"You're an honest man, Tanger. You're willing to stick your neck out and help me find Emma. I ask because friends confide in friends, that's why."

Tanger took a bite of his chicken as he looked away for a moment. After a few minutes he spoke. "Yeah, I suppose so. I was nineteen when my dad died. We were traveling West, and my mom took sick with the fever, too, but she lived. We had hardly put my dad in the ground and marked his grave when my uncle took some of the supplies and gear and rode off. He left me alone to take care of my mom and to finish the trip. I've never seen him since, and I don't care to."

"Is he the one that you're named after?" Will pressed.

"You have a way about you, don't you! It must be the lawman in you. My first name is Eric, and I'm named after my dad's older brother, the one who left me and my mother to survive on our own. My uncle traveled with us when my dad was alive, but he changed as fast as the wind does."

"That must've been hard for you. But is holding on to this anger doing you any good? What have you gained by it, Tanger? Do you think it's hurting your uncle any?"

"He doesn't care a lick for us. He's probably living a good life somewhere, but he only cares for himself. He's an old fool!"

"Tanger, you should be proud of your name, because your folks gave it to you. Eric is a good strong name!" Will added forcibly.

"Why am I telling you this anyway? All it does is get me irritated."

"Maybe it's time, Tanger. Maybe it's time to let go."

Tanger quickly changed the subject. "I don't want Marie Rose's chicken wasted, so eat up!" He grabbed another piece for himself and then jumped up and walked over to his horse.

Yann looked at Will as if to say "What do you make of that?" but they didn't speak. They both sat quietly. Yann then lay back and stared up at the stars. His mind was full of thoughts as he compared his predicament with Will's situation. *Will has more courage and strength than I. He's willing to die for the one he loves, yet I'm running from my own war. It's shameful. Is Sanne of less value than his wife? Are his enemies greater than mine? No, they cannot be! I must become free from these men, and somehow I must have Sanne by my side.* With deep conviction Yann decided then and there that he needed to face his problem head-on.

Yann wasn't the only one lost in thought. Will's mind raced again as he sat by the fire thinking of what had transpired since Emma had been kidnapped. So many changes had occurred since the beginning of his journey. So many of the changes were answers to prayer—the seashell was just one example. He was still amazed at how God had led Emma to the trading post and given her the opportunity to leave him the seashell.

As he thought about the seashell, it dawned on him as to why Emma had it with her. A few minutes before leaving for the job interview, he had found the shell on the floor. It usually sat on the windowsill in the front room by the rocking chair, but he didn't place it back on the windowsill. Instead, he handed it to Emma for safekeeping. She commented that she'd put it back later, but for the moment Emma had stuck it in the pocket of the work dress she was wearing. If Loretta hadn't played with the shell and if he hadn't handed it to Emma after picking it up and if she hadn't placed it in her pocket, the shell could not have been used as a sign. *God works in such simple ways that are often times hidden from man's sight,* Will thought.

Yann's voice suddenly pierced the air. "It's Seen! Now I know who's after me. He's a master and will be difficult to stop, but I will no longer run from him."

"He's the man you couldn't identify? It's good to know your enemies. I wish I knew mine better," commented Will.

"Some of the things you have said have given me much to think about. When I compare myself with your willingness to die for what you believe and what is dear to you, I feel ashamed. So I've decided that I'm finished running."

"Now your life can begin again. You can't hide from yourself. We have to face our lives and deal with what is given to us, but we do become better for it."

"I'm starting to see that," Yann said.

"How are you going to stop him, Yann? Do you need our help?" Will asked.

"I'm going to continue to ride with you until he finds me, and he will find me, that I guarantee."

"Are you going to try and kill him?" Will asked.

"When Seen finds me, one or both of us will die. There is no other way," he answered matter-of-factly.

"I do think there is another way, but it depends on what you believe. Have you decided what you believe?"

"No."

"If you give the Lord the opportunity, He will show you what to do."

"I'm still confused. Right now I need to be alone with my thoughts. I'm gonna go sleep behind the pines." Yann stood up and walked away with his bedroll.

Will watched him disappear into the darkness, praying that Yann would find peace and surrender his will to God. Will's mind then turned to his own thoughts and the war raging with his own doubts. *It's like a beast that stocks you each step of the way until doubt triumphs or the soul surrenders to faith,* he thought. The fire was burning low, so Will tossed on a few pieces of wood. He then stretched out and went to sleep.

ॐॐॐॐॐॐ

Will woke with the morning light and a few early birds singing. He stood up and kicked the bottom of one of Tanger's moccasins and said, "Time to rise, Tanger." As Will started a fire, Tanger picked up his gear.

"Where's Yann?"

"He bedded down behind the pines over there," Will said without looking up.

"What's for breakfast?" Tanger asked.

"I don't know, but it has to be quick."

"While you figure it out, I'll get Yann," Tanger said.

The next thing Will heard as he rummaged through the supplies was "Will, come here quick! Yann's gone. Something happened."

Will ran over to find Yann's bedroll still spread out on the ground.

"Someone rode off with Yann and didn't ask permission. Look here, he was dragged, then picked up and carried to a horse. I can tell because the boot prints become deeper from Yann's weight. He tied him to the horse here. See the prints on both sides of the horse tracks? The horse was in this position. They headed south," Tanger said as he carefully surveyed the tracks.

"It's Seen. He took Yann back to San Francisco," Will said.

"Seen?" Tanger said.

"Yann figured out last night who was chasing him. He's someone Yann knows from China."

"We ought to go after him. I'm sure he could use our help."

"I don't want to leave him stranded, but just last night he told me he needed to do this on his own and that he was done running. I think he's prepared to take care of Seen on his own. I hope he'll be back, but I can't wait. I'm going for Emma; I think that's what Yann would want me to do. You can go look for him or come with me; it's your choice." Will moved away from Tanger and picked up Yann's bedroll. "I'm gonna go eat. I want to reach Fort Reading by noon."

❦❦❦❦❦

Tanger decided to stick with Will and search for Emma, but his thoughts were on their abducted friend as they rode across the terrain before them. After a hard morning's ride, Fort Reading looked welcoming. The fort sat on about ten acres along the banks of Cow Creek, but it didn't have any walls or gates. Spread out across the grounds were officers' quarters, barracks, a kitchen, a storehouse, a hospital, a carpenter's shop, a bakery, and a fine stable, along with a few other buildings.

The creek provided the fort with drinking water, cold summer baths, and fresh fish, but when the rains came, the grounds looked more like a small lake than a military post. At the water's highest point of the season, the men would build bridges to go between the buildings. Sickness was common among the soldiers with intermittent fever troubling them the most. Under these conditions, it was difficult to be an effective soldier, but these conditions were hidden from view during the dry season, which was just in its beginning stages for the year. They rode up and dismounted in front of the stable, which they both agreed would be a likely place to start asking questions since the building was frequented by the soldiers. As they entered, they found a young private cleaning stalls by himself. They proceeded to ask him if he had seen or heard anything about the three kidnappers and Emma.

"Nope, I haven't seen a thing, and I've heard nothing from nobody, but I sure hope you find her real soon. I'll keep an eye out for them," he said. "I'd check with the group of wagons on the north side of the fort. Maybe someone has seen the ones you're lookin' for; they just came in two day ago."

Will and Tanger thanked him and moved on.

The assembly of wagons numbered fifteen in all. Will and Tanger split up so as to cover more ground and offer a sense of privacy to their conversations. A young man and his wife told Tanger that they had come down from Oregon City. After arriving in Oregon last fall, they decided among themselves that the Oregon territory wasn't suitable to their liking. The group decided that California, near Los Angeles, was a better location to settle. The same basic story was repeated again and again.

Finally Tanger came across a woman who had seen three men and a woman hurriedly heading north. The men fit the basic description that Marie Rose had given them, one tall and two shorter. Tanger was excited to tell Will the news. He weaved his way through the wagons, looking for his partner. A woman suddenly stopped Tanger. "Are you looking for the man whose wife was kidnapped? The poor soul; I hope he finds her."

"Which way did he go?"

She raised her arm and pointed to his left. "Your friend walked straight toward those wagons, and I haven't seen him since."

"Thanks," Tanger replied.

As he approached the cluster of wagons, he noticed a small group of people crowded together. He then felt that something was wrong, so he ran over to the group. Everyone seemed to be talking all at once. "Who would do such a thing?" "He looks dead to me." "What did he do anyway?"

Tanger asked a few of the people to step aside so he could see who the unfortunate person was that they were talking about. To his amazement, he looked down at Will who was half under one of the wagons, his head covered with blood. Tanger quickly knelt down next to him. He did appear dead; he had been badly beaten, also booted. Tanger put his ear to his chest; he could hear a heartbeat, which gave him hope. Anger filled him almost to the point of seeing red. The men who had done this would have received the same treatment if they had been within Tanger's reach. He stood up and addressed the crowd in a loud voice, "Did anyone see this happen?"

He then squatted down and pulled Will from under the wagon, sliding his arms under him and carefully lifting him up. A woman stepped out of the crowd, and without being asked, said, "Bring him to my wagon. I'll take care of him!"

"Would you pick up my rifle?" Tanger asked. The woman complied and gestured with her right hand to follow her.

He followed her to a larger than average wagon. She climbed in and directed Tanger to put Will in head first while she took hold of his shoulders and helped pull him in. At that moment a boy who looked to be about eight years old appeared beside Tanger. "Do you need any help, Mom?"

"Yes, Clay, I need water from the barrel and a few clean towels if there are any, and hurry, son!"

"Thanks for the help ... for taking him in. By the way, my name is Tanger."

The woman nodded her head and then said, "I'm Kate. I wasn't able to save my husband's life, but maybe I can help save this man. He's unconscious, and his right eye and mouth look terrible. I've got to get him out of these clothes. Son, hurry up!"

"Coming, Mom. I'm just getting a towel. I found a good rag, too!"

"That will help, son," she said.

Before Tanger could say another word, a short older man appeared and said, "It happened at my wagon. I couldn't stop it. One of them said they'd do the same to me if I spoke up."

"What's their names, and where are they?" There was a coldness in his voice. "I said, what's their names?" Tanger stated with authority.

"Perkins and Whipple; Perkins is the tall one. Their wagon is somewhere in the group, but I don't know where. Perkins is trouble, lots of trouble, and they called this man," pointing to Will, "Tatterfield," the older man answered.

"They won't be trouble much longer," Tanger promised.

Clay handed his mom the water, towel, and rag before jumping down from the wagon and running off to the nearest wagon next to theirs.

"Tanger! Before you go running off, tell me who am I taking care of. Who is this man?" Kate asked.

Tanger stuck his head in the wagon and said, "His name is Will Jacobs, and he's my partner." He then turned to the older man and said, "Help her by doing whatever she tells you to do."

He then turned to search for the assailants. Max was at Tanger's side by the time he stopped at the first wagon. He started his search with the simple question, "I'm looking for Whipple and Perkins." At the third wagon a young woman with a little girl clinging to her side responded. "Their wagon is the one over there with the canvas drawn up."

"Thank you!" Tanger said.

As he walked toward their wagon, he cradled his rifle and tried to think of a way to handle this situation without hurting them too much. He was still plenty mad. In the short time since he agreed to ride with Will, he felt a brotherly bond, and Tanger never took it lightly when someone troubled his family. He walked past their wagon and told Max to stay. He then approached them from behind.

"Are you two Whipple and Perkins?"

They both turned in surprise to see who was asking. Perkins spoke first. "What are you doin' sneaking up on us like that, and who's askin' anyway?"

"I'm not sneaking, that's what happens when a man wears moccasins. I thought I'd congratulate you two for just about beatin' that man to death. He must've really rubbed you two the wrong way. What's his name, Tatterfield, or something like that?"

"Yeah, it's Tatterfield, all right. He's a useless liar and thief. I vowed to Whipple and myself that the next time I met up with him I'd get what he owed me one way or another," Perkins said, shaking his fist in the air.

"So you and Whipple decided that taking care of Tatterfield would make this world a better place for all of us. Why don't you two just—"

Perkins cut him off, "Look! He came overland with the group of us, and one morning he just disappeared. My pistol and holster along with a good skinning knife and the best pair of boots I've ever owned disappeared with him. So I think this pistol and holster kind of evens things up a little bit," Perkins said with a sense of satisfaction.

"Why so many questions, and why is Tatterfield so important to you anyway?" Whipple asked nervously.

"Tell me what the initials on the front of the holster stand for, Perkins?" Tanger asked as he shifted his weight to his right foot.

"It don't matter! He must of stole it from someone like he did mine," he answered.

"It's got W. J. tooled in it! That stands for Will Jacobs, the sheriff of Stone Ridge south of here, who happens to be the man I'm riding with. So hand over his gun," ordered Tanger.

"What! You're ridin' with him! Then you must be just like him because skunks stick with their own kind. I'm not giving up this gun."

"Perkins! I've been real patient with you, but accusing me on top of nearly killing my partner is as far as this is going to go." He stepped forward, pushing the end of the rifle barrel against Perkins chest and pulling back the hammer. He then said, "Unbuckle the holster and drop it."

Perkins could no longer argue the point. He unbuckled it and let it slip from his fingers to the ground.

Tanger stepped back and said, "Kick it to me."

Perkins said nothing; he just obeyed.

"That's the first intelligent thing I've seen you do, Perkins," Tanger said with a slight grin.

Whipple was hoping to quietly disappear as all this was going on, but Tanger noticed his slight movement. "Max, come!" Max came out from under the wagon where he had been hiding. "Whipple, take a good look at my dog. He has just enough wolf in him to have you for his next meal, and he will if I tell him to, so stay put!"

"Here you are, Tanger!" Kate said as she ran up from behind him. "Look at this; he's a sheriff! I found this badge in his shirt pocket. Are these the men that beat him?"

"Hold the badge up so they can see it real clear," Tanger said. "Perkins, don't you ever call me a liar again because if there's a next time I won't take you to the lieutenant like I'm going to do this time."

"Kate, pick up the sheriff's gun and holster," Tanger said. "Let's go see the lieutenant, you two. I think he's going to find this very interesting. Perkins, you lead the way," he ordered.

Kate did what she was told, but she stopped Tanger before he got too far. "You had better take these things with you. The lieutenant will want to see them. I'm going back to look after Will. My son is watching him now."

Kate handed Tanger the gun and holster and turned back toward her wagon. Tanger marched the two men off toward the lieutenant's office. They caught the eyes of many. The sight of Tanger, all six feet four inches of him, was reminiscent of days gone by—the days of mountain men in buckskins, moccasins, raccoon caps, and other assorted mountaineering equipment. Some people looked on while others followed.

Reaching the lieutenant's office, Tanger ordered, "Perkins, knock on the door." A moment later the door opened and there stood the lieutenant, commander of Co. E, 2nd infantry. Tanger immediately spoke up, "I want these men arrested."

"I'm Lieutenant Hadley. Come in, and let's discuss it." Before shutting the door, he said, "Private, get Sergeant Banning and have him come to my office at once."

"The first question, sir, is who are you, and why am I arresting these men?" the lieutenant asked.

"I'm Tanger. I live north of here, and these two men almost beat to death Sheriff Will Jacobs of Stone Ridge, a town below Marysville. Lieutenant, here's the gun and holster they stole from him, and here is the sheriff's badge, which we found in his pocket." Tanger placed them on the lieutenant's desk.

"Did you see this happen?"

"No, but I can bring you the man who did," Tanger answered.

The lieutenant turned to the accused men and asked, "Is it true what this man is saying?"

Perkins answered. "Yeah it is, but we didn't know he was a sheriff. We thought he was Tatterfield who stole from us last fall comin' overland. We wouldn't have done it if we knew he was a lawman."

There was a knock on the door. The lieutenant said, "Banning?"

"Yes, sir, it is," was the response.

"Come in, sergeant. These two men are under arrest. Put them in the guardhouse. I'll have more details for you later."

"Yes, sir!" The sergeant drew his pistol and pointing to the door. "You two men, outside and do it peaceably."

The lieutenant had picked up the badge and was rolling it over and under his fingers like some old card shark. "I'd like to see the sheriff and talk to the witness. I'll walk back with you," the lieutenant stated.

They left the office and in no time were looking in Kate's wagon as she was putting a cool cloth on Will's head. She looked up and asked, "How did it go? Were they arrested?"

"Yes, I'll tell you about it later. This is Lieutenant Hadley; he's in charge here."

"I'm Kate Weissman."

"It's nice to meet you, Miss Weissman. Are you the one who found the badge?" the lieutenant asked.

"Yes, I found the badge in his top pocket. Please come take a look at him so you can see how bad the beating was." Lieutenant Hadley climbed in and found a place to kneel next to her.

"When I looked him over, I didn't find any broken bones. If there are any cracked ones, I can't tell. He was unconscious, but he came out of it a little while ago. He's asleep now. He was hit in the back of the head and near his right eye. I've stitched up his face and head where needed, but he lost half a tooth in front and I'm concerned about his right eye. He was hit terribly hard on that side," Kate stated.

"Have you had medical training? You've done a fine job with him," the lieutenant commented.

"Some, my brother is a doctor back East. I worked with him for a time," she answered.

"I've seen enough. Thank you, Miss Weissman. Tanger, I need to talk to the witness."

"Follow me," Tanger replied.

After a few minutes walk, Tanger said, "I'm going to leave you here lieutenant; this is where it all happened. The witness is the older man with the whitish hair talking to the redheaded woman."

Tanger checked on the horses and then headed back to see Will. As he approached the wagon, he found Kate standing by the water barrel washing her face and hands. For the first time he noticed that she was an attractive woman. She stood about six foot tall and had light brown hair.

"Hi, Kate."

"Hi, is your business with the lieutenant done?"

"Yeah, it is. The rest is up to Will. How is he doing?"

"He lifted his head for a moment, but I'm sure it's pounding with pain. Fortunately, it's a good sign that he's going to make it," she said.

"Has he said anything yet? I need to talk to him."

"No, and I'd think with his mouth as it is he won't be for awhile. I'd like him to drink some water if he could."

"Let me give it a try." He climbed in the wagon, but Will appeared to be asleep. Nevertheless, he picked up the cup of water and tried to rouse him. "Will, it's me, Tanger, are you awake? I'd like you to drink a little of this water. I don't want you to die on me."

Will opened his one good eye.

"How do you feel?"

"I ache," he said without moving his lips.

"I have an idea," Tanger said. He picked up a clean piece of cloth that sat by the water bucket and poured some water from the cup onto it. He then proceeded to squeeze water into Will's mouth from the cloth. That would suffice until he was able to use a cup.

"Will, Kate is the woman who's taking care of you. She said you don't have any broken bones, but you've been beaten pretty bad. She stitched up your head and face. I'm sure you are in a lot of pain, but I have a few things to tell you. Perkins and Whipple are the two men who beat you. I had them arrested. They're in the guardhouse, and they admitted to doing it. They thought you were a man named Tatterfield who stole from them, so it was done in revenge. It's going to be a few days or so till you're ready to ride again.

"This beating is like a cog in the wheel, but it's just a delay. We will be heading out soon, and that's a promise, Will. Let me squeeze a little more water in your mouth, then you can rest. I'll check on you later." He finished up and climbed out of the wagon. As his feet hit the ground, he noticed Kate sitting by the side of the wagon.

"I was listening. You did a good job," she stated. "By the way, are you hungry? If you are, could you build me a fire?"

"Yes, I am, and yes, I will." He pulled a leather tie from his bag and tied back his hair. He eyed a small pile of wood near the fire pit. He stepped over to it and was surprised to find a few coals hiding under the ashes. With just a handful of twigs, he was able to quickly restart the fire, and he had it blazing in minutes.

Tanger grabbed the short stool that Kate had been using and sat down by the fire to tend it. As he sat there, his mind wandered. *I wonder how Yann is doing. Is he alive? Will we see him again? And what about Will? We were making progress, but now we've come to a grinding halt.* He sat wondering what the outcome would be to all of this. He knew he sure didn't have any answers.

"Would you take the pot that's hanging on the wagon and fill it with water about three quarters full, Tanger?" Kate asked in a manner that implied that she was a little edgy.

He got up and did as he was asked, then he added a little more wood to the fire before putting the pot on it.

Kate added a bowl of cut dry vegetables to the boiling water. The soup and wheat bread she had were going to make a tasty meal. "I'll ask Clay to go fishing tomorrow. Having fresh fish for supper would be nice, and he doesn't look at fishing as work; it's just fun he says. If you like you can go to the river with him."

"Yeah, I like to fish too." Tanger sat in silence for a moment before he broached the topic that was on his mind. "Kate, when you asked me to get the pot for the soup, you seemed edgy. Is something wrong? Did I do anything to upset you?"

"This is all very reminiscent of my husband's death. I tried to save him after the accident, but I couldn't. He died the next day."

"What kind of accident was it?"

"My husband tried to stop a runaway buggy, but instead of stopping the spooked horse, the buggy and horse ran over him. He was badly hurt, and there was nothing I could do to save him. That's what everyone told me, but sometimes I don't believe it."

"Sometimes all we can do is our best. When my dad died of the fever coming overland, my ma helped me to understand that I did all I could do." Their short and intimate talk was interrupted by Clay's appearance.

"Where have you been, son?" Kate asked as Clay walked up to them.

54

Clay smelled the soup and commented, "I'm hungry, Mom. Can I eat?"

"Where did you go, Clay?"

"Just over to that wagon to play with my new friend. His name is Albert."

"Next time please tell me where you are going. Now, in answer to your question, we will eat soon. Go wash up and get the bowls and spoons please."

"I'm going to check on Will," Kate said as she stood up and walked to the rear of the wagon.

Clay returned and handed Tanger a bowl and spoon. He then stood silently looking him over. Tanger respected his choice to stare and said nothing. A moment later Clay took a step forward and began peppering him with questions. "Where'd you get the leather clothes? How far can you throw that knife? Can I have some Indian moccasins like you have?"

He stopped to take a breath, and Tanger took the opportunity to answer him. "I made these clothes and moccasins, and I can make you a pair of moccasins if I can get the leather. There's nothing like moccasins for the feet. Your ma said she wants us to go fishing tomorrow for supper." Tanger reached over and took the pot off the fire.

Clay's face lit up with excitement as he said, "You'll go fishin' with me and make me moccasins, too! Thanks!"

Out of the corner of his eye, Tanger saw Kate climb out of the wagon. He stood and turned toward her as she approached him. "He's sleeping well, and he doesn't have a fever, which is a good sign. He's going to need more water later. And let's save some of the juice from the soup because I know he's going be very hungry when he wakes up."

"Mom, can we eat? I'm hungry."

"Yes, sit down and I'll serve you."

After eating, checking on the horses, and going to the river so Clay could show Tanger his best fishing spots, which then led to a little exploring for bigger and better fishing up river, Tanger was ready to turn in. It had been an exhausting day.

ざぐ ぐ ぐ ぐ ぐ

It was about mid-morning the next day when Tanger and Clay got back from fishing and began cleaning their fresh catch. Kate was rummaging through the side box of the wagon for a few misplaced items when she heard

Will say something that was undistinguishable. She hurriedly headed for the back of the wagon.

Tanger wasn't far behind her. "Keep up the good work, Clay. I'll be back in a minute to help you," he said.

When he reached the wagon, he found Kate kneeling beside Will. "He wants to sit up. Can you help me prop him up?"

Tanger carefully climbed in, trying not to knock anything over or step on Will for what room was left was all but gone. As they sat him up and leaned him against an old wooden chest, a few groans came from deep within him.

"Are you ready to eat something?" Kate asked. Will moved his head, signifying yes.

"Good, that's what I wanted to hear. I'll get the soup and be right back," she said.

"Hurts a lot; stiff all over," Will uttered.

"Can you raise your arms and bend your legs?" Tanger questioned.

Will slowly raised both arms over his head and put them down again to rest flat on the wagons floor; he then drew his left and right leg toward his chest. The right leg was much more painful than the left. The bruise above his right knee showed the reason for the extra pain—a large bruise had appeared that could have come from the heel of a boot.

Tanger smiled and shook his head. "You're a tough man, Will. It's gonna take more than a beating to stop you. Now how do you feel?"

Will remained silent, letting the question go.

"Let's be optimistic," Tanger said. "It could be worse; you could be dead." Kate reappeared with the soup. She handed the cup and spoon to Tanger and turned to address Will. "It's barely warm, but if you can drink it, it will be a good start. We're having boiled fish tonight for dinner. You need to get your strength back, so please drink up."

Will wanted to feed himself, so he carefully took the cup and spoon from Tanger and gingerly put the spoon to his mouth. He could feel his upper lip throb as he tried to suck the soup off the spoon, but it tasted good so he continued on with a second spoonful.

"Lieutenant Hadley is going to want to talk to you about all of this when you're up to it. It's up to you to press charges, but you probably already know that. If I was you, Will, I'd give 'um an equal beating in return, but I'm not you," Tanger said

"Help me to the edge of the wagon," Will said in a low voice.

"Watch yourself, you took a hard blow on the head. I don't want you to pass out."

"Just help me," Will said.

Tanger was trying to figure out the easiest way to move Will without inflicting too much pain. He decided to slide Will across the floor of the wagon, so he pushed the chest back and gently helped Will lay back down. Then Tanger slowly pulled Will by the feet to the edge of the wagon where he helped him into an upright position. In spite of the pain, Will was grateful to be sitting up and looking around.

"I'll get you more soup," Tanger said when Will finished the first cup.

They must've hit me really hard because I can't see out of my right eye, he thought to himself. He then moved his head around. *Thank you, Lord, that my neck is all right.*

Max got up from where he was lying and came up to Will. He proceeded to rub his head against Will's legs as they hung down from the wagon's edge. Will thought it would be a good thing to have a dog like Max.

Tanger returned with Kate and the second cup of soup. As he handed it over to Will, he commented, "I was just thinking about Yann. I wonder how he's doing; hopefully better than you."

"Yeah, I don't know," Will replied with difficulty. He exhaled a lung full of air, which helped release a little bit of his built-up stress. His upper lip started to throb more intensely, which put an end to the almost nonexistent conversation. His mind drifted off to more pressing matters. *How many days will I be delayed because of this.*

Kate broke through his troubled thoughts. "Will, do you know that you're a miracle? To be beaten as badly as you were and not have a broken bone or more serious harm done to your head is a miracle. God has plans for you. You're eating and sitting up just a day later; you're doing remarkably well."

Will handed the cup back to Kate; he couldn't finish it, and he needed to lie down before he tipped over. With their aid he lay back and immediately felt a little more comfortable. Before falling asleep, he prayed fervently to the Lord. *Please heal me soon, Lord. Help me find Emma. I need Your strength to finish this. I hurt all over, Lord. Heal me, please!*

৵৵৵৵৵

Four days passed quickly. They were filled with Kate's good cooking and plenty of rest and healing. Will felt amazingly stronger. His pounding head no longer ached and his right eye was showing some signs of improvement—he could actually see out of it a wee bit. As they all sat and ate by the wagon, Will said, "I'll be done in a minute, then I'm saddling Bella and going for a short ride. You want to join me, Tanger?"

"Yeah, I think the horses can use the ride, too."

It was a clear day with blue skies above; it was already warm, which hinted at a hot afternoon. They rode east past the fort through wooded and open areas as they followed Cow Creek. It was obvious that the fort was definitely built in the wrong location. Will could see signs of past flooding along the creek with high watermarks on trees, and there were areas of erosion many yards over its present banks.

"I'm going to see the men in the guardhouse when we get back. It's time to finish up business and head out in the morning. I feel up to it. This ride feels good even though my right leg still aches."

They rode on in silence for a little longer, and then Will broached a topic he had been wanting to discuss with Tanger ever since he had been well enough to sit up and observe Kate and Tanger. "Tanger, I can see that you and Kate favor each other, and I don't want to be the one responsible for interfering with such things, so feel free to stay behind, if you like."

"I don't have an inkling of what you're talking about," Tanger replied with a very straight face.

"Have it your way, my friend. I know what I see, and she's a good, capable woman, but I'll say no more."

As they rode back to the wagon, Tanger asked, "Do you want me to tag along with you to the guardhouse?"

"No, I'll go alone. It will be better that way. I also have to write the report for the lieutenant, so I'll be a while." Will felt the desire to pick up the pace and see how it would affect his leg, so he rode on ahead.

A private was standing guard by the one and only door to the guardhouse as Will approached.

"Private."

"Yes, sir, what do you need?"

"I'm Will Jacobs; I need to speak to the two men you're holding. I have a few questions for them. The lieutenant knows I'm here."

The private pulled open the door, which allowed the light to drive out some of the darkness. Each cell had just one small barred window for light and fresh air. Will entered to find both the men in the first cell on the left. He stood in front of the cell door and said, "So you're the two men. Which one of you is Perkins?"

Perkins got up from his cot and moved toward the cell door. "We must not of beat you too badly; you look like you're getting along pretty well, but you still look like Tatterfield to me."

Will ignored the comment and looked over at the other man who was still sitting. "You're Whipple, aren't you? Tell me, what did you hit me with?"

Whipple didn't raise his head. He just continued looking down at the floor as he said, "I used a broken wheel spoke off our wagon. Sorry about hitting you, I was kinda talked into it. I know Tatterfield did wrong, but beating a man like we beat you is not my way. I know we're in deep trouble with you being on the right side of the law as you are. What are you and the lieutenant going to do with us?"

"First thing, you're going to give Miss Weissman fifty dollars each for her time, food, and medicine that she used taking care of me. And I'll tell you, you're both fortunate that Tanger didn't give you an equal beating in return, because he's more than capable of doing it."

"That remains to be seen. I don't know if he's that tough," Perkins said with a sneer.

Will looked him in the eye as he said, "You're a hateful man, Perkins, and I'd be real careful if I was you. I don't know what the lieutenant is going to do. This is his post not mine." He turned and headed for the lieutenant's office.

After being ushered into the lieutenant's office and given a seat, the lieutenant said, "So tell me what you think about the two of them."

"My thoughts are mixed, lieutenant. Whipple apologized and said he was the one who hit me with a broken wheel spoke. I'd give him less time. Perkins on the other hand is a hard man. I didn't see an ounce of remorse in him. I think he'd do it again, just for spite. I'd give him the maximum time to sit and think, but I'll leave the matter to you."

"I can give Perkins ninety days, that's it. The law won't allow any more than that for the crime."

"I'm satisfied with that, lieutenant. I told them that I expect fifty dollars each to be paid to Miss Weissman for the medicine and care she gave me. Is that acceptable?"

"With the way prices are today, fifty dollars a piece for medical attention is a bargain. I'll collect the fine and see that Miss Weissman receives it. I'm going to need a sworn statement from you in the next day or two so I can officially charge the two of them. I already have one from the eyewitness."

"I'm going to write it up now, lieutenant."

"If it will make it easier, you can use my desk. I have paper and pen here," the lieutenant said. "And by the way, Will, I'm glad you're showing signs of a good recovery."

"Thank you. So am I." Will moved to sit behind the desk and write the report. He was ready to move on.

હજ્ય હજ્ય હજ્ય

"Kate, it looks like we're leaving in the morning," Tanger said when he returned to camp.

"I thought you would be. He's healing nicely, but he needs your help still. Make sure you take good care of him and yourself."

"When will you be heading to Los Angeles?" asked Tanger.

"I'm not. The lieutenant asked me to assist in the hospital. We get a place to stay, and I'm paid. I'm looking forward to moving out of this wagon. It's a job for the time being until a better opportunity arrives, and Clay loves the river and the area. Does Clay know you're leaving?"

"No, I didn't tell him yet."

"He's taken a liking to you. You're the first man since his father died that he's opened up to."

"I like Clay; he's a good boy, Kate."

"Tanger, can I ask you what your first name is? Wouldn't it be a kind thing to tell me?" she said.

Tanger paused for a second before answering. "My given name is Eric Isaac Tanger."

"Was that so hard to do?" she asked.

"Yes and no," he said. "For years I've hidden some things about my life, but maybe it's time to let go."

"There's no reason to hide things from me, is there?" she said as she looked into his brown eyes.

"I guess not," he answered.

Tanger turned his attention from Kate as Will approached.

"I'm done with my report, and the lieutenant is satisfied. Kate, you are going to receive one hundred dollars for taking care of me."

"One hundred dollars? From who?" she said with a surprised look.

"It's the generous contribution of Perkins and Whipple. It's a fine that they owe and that you have rightly earned," Will stated.

"Thank you. It will help."

"Kate, you've done more than I can express in words. I'm thankful for your care and friendship." Will then turned to Tanger. "Let's be ready to ride at daybreak. As you've said, I'm itchin' to go."

"I'll be ready, Will."

"I can put some food together for the two of you," Kate stated.

"I'm still going to push north on the main road and not take the pass. That's what I feel impressed to do," Will said.

"That's what we decided before you got hit on the head. Did you forget?"

"I kind of did. I wasn't hit with a feather you know," Will retorted.

"I forgive ya for that," Tanger said with a one-sided smile. "I'm headed over to check on the horses and then start packing the gear. Why don't you join me, sheriff?

"Yeah, the sheriff would like that."

ৰ৵ৰ৵ৰ৵ৰ৵ৰ৵

The sun didn't disappoint Will's plans to start at daybreak—it came up on time. Kate got breakfast ready as the men saddled and loaded their supplies. Clay was busy asking a dozen questions, and Max was underfoot, knowing that something was up.

"Food's ready!" they heard Kate say. Everyone eagerly sat down and ate in relative silence. Will sensed awkwardness between Tanger and Kate that hovered over each of them. Will kept his thoughts to himself because it really wasn't any of his business. As they finished up, Will thanked Kate once again for her care. "I want Emma to meet you on the way home. We'll stop in."

"We need to get started while the day is fresh," Tanger interjected.

Will mounted Bella as Tanger moved slowly toward his horse.

"Eric Isaac Tanger, stop!"

Kate's command stopped Tanger dead in his tracks. He turned around and faced her. "What is it, Kate?"

"I know you have feelings. I can tell," she said. "Do you think I took this job just because I like taking care of sick soldiers? I need to know if you are coming back?" she said. "I need to know if I should stay or leave."

"I didn't know how you felt, so I said nothing. This is all new to me. Yes, I'm coming back."

A sense of relief flooded over Kate as she felt tears well up in her eyes. "I was hoping you'd say that."

Before mounting his horse, Tanger pulled the bluebird feather out of his cap. He stepped closer to her and said, "This is a small reminder of me that I want you to keep. I love the deep blue feathers of the bluebirds. They are beautiful like you."

She accepted the feather and then put her hand on his arm. "I'll be here when you return. You'd better go now, Eric Tanger, and be safe."

"I will," he said with a smile. For once he felt peace in his heart. As he walked toward his horse, he stopped at Clay's side. Giving the boy's right shoulder a squeeze, he said, "I'll be back again, and we'll go fishing and do other things. Take care of your mom until then, OK?"

"I will. Come back soon," Clay said in return as Tanger mounted his horse.

As they rode off, Tanger looked over at Will and said, "Don't you say a word, my friend!"

Will just smiled a little and tried not to laugh—his upper lip would not thank him if he did so.

Chapter Five

The Escape

Yann closed his eyes. He thought it would be easier than staring at the moving ground. His chest and gut ached from being tied across the back of Seen's extra mount. He now understood what it would be like to be a bag of grain on the back of a mule. Seen threw out insults that he hadn't used before—about how Yann was so poorly trained, that it was a simple thing to find and capture him, that he was a child and it was amazing that he was even accepted as a guard, and that he wasn't qualified to guard the governor's dogs.

It had been hours since Yann had been hit over the head and tied to the horse's back. The pain he felt had become one large ache, and with every step of the horse, he was reminded of it. He could see the plan. If he was starved, made stiff from being tied to the horse, and subjected to put downs, he could be rendered useless—not a threat.

As he was thinking about these things, Seen abruptly stopped and climbed down from his horse. Yann braced himself for another painful blow to the head, but it didn't come. Seen walked around to the left side of the horse and untied Yann's feet, while leaving his hands still tied. Yann took this opportunity to swing his legs up and over the back of the horse in hopes of landing on his feet. Seen anticipated his move, and with a quick jerk of the rope, he pulled Yann's arms up against the horse's side just as his feet touched the ground.

The horse lunged forward in surprise, almost knocking Yann off his feet. Seen then moved to the back of the horse as he pulled Yann sideways, forcing him to lose his balance. Yann lay motionless on the ground, feeling that his strength was spent. He hoped he could just lie there and rest.

The rope became painfully tight as Seen jerked it once again and said, "Now walk, you foolish dog!" Seen took the reins of the extra horse, and mounting his own, pulled Yann to his feet. Seen covered Yann with insults, yet he understood that Yann was a skillful man. He had to be to have held the position of personal bodyguard for the governor of such a large province.

Until now they had traveled off the main road so as not to attract attention. Seen now turned west down a dry wash that led to the wagon road. Yann thought about the promise he had made to himself that he was finished running—now his test had come. The rest of the conversation by the fireside also came to mind. He had been affected by the words that Will spoke just the night before. He needed to put to rest the doubts and confusion he felt over God.

He struggled to keep his balance as he ran and walked through the brush along the path they were taking, some with sharp thorns and others with dead and dried branches that could puncture the skin like a dull knife. He fell a few times only to be insulted and then pulled back to his feet. Yann could hear in the near distance the voice of a man hollering at his mules, and he knew the main road was just up ahead. Just then Yann lost his footing once again and fell face first. With his hands tied, the best he could do was to turn his face to one side.

Lying face down in the wash with rocks and stones for a bed, he could feel the jab of a sharp-edged stone in his side. "Get to your feet!" Seen yelled. When Yann didn't move, Seen dragged him about a yard before stopping. Yann's hand rested on a palm-sized stone in his right hand. He took hold of it as he struggled to his feet.

To Yann's surprise, he was led back up the hill away from the main road. They ascended at an angle to the tree line. The trees were overgrown, with just enough room left between them to weave their way through like ants walking in the tall grass. He felt relieved as they moved out of the overgrown woods to an area more sparsely covered with brush and smaller trees. Steps turned into miles and minutes into hours as he was pulled along with no more freedom than the horse he walked behind.

A small tunnel through the woods showed that a trail was up ahead, offering the promise of shade and some cool air. His legs were weak, and his mouth was hot and dry. He needed rest, food, and water. His step became a little lighter as they approached the trail—he anticipated the path to be easier.

Once in the shade of the trees, Seen stopped and dismounted. He turned to Yann and said, "Even to cowards and murderers, China shows mercy. You can rest and drink water." Seen took one of his extra canteens and threw it at Yann's feet. Yann sat down, picked it up, quickly opened it, and took a long drink.

"I don't want you to think about getting comfortable. You thought we were going to take the wagon road, didn't you? Do you now see that your suffering has just begun? I'm going to keep you alive until we reach China where you will stand before the governor to be condemned and to have your head removed. That will give me great joy, and your sweet Sanne will never be your wife. Another man will have her."

No other words could have hurt more deeply than those. It only strengthened his desire to be free; he must find Seen's weakness and escape. He hadn't spoken a word since he was captured the night before. There was no real need to; it wouldn't accomplish a thing. The nagging rope was cutting into his wrist. He desperately wanted to remove it.

Seen sat down and leaned against a tree approximately twenty feet away. He focused his attention on a small patch of blue sky that was peeking through the tops of the trees. This gave Yann the opportunity to use the stone he still held in his hand to try to cut the rope. The way his wrists were tied together made it difficult to cut the strands of rope, but in spite of the odds he was making headway.

After awhile Seen stood up and stroked the top of his smoothly shaved head with his left hand. He stretched his arms and legs before moving toward his horse. As he moved, he gave the rope a hard jerk. "Your rest is over, Yann Chang," he said. He mounted his horse and started to ride off, pulling the rope tight and giving Yann little time to put the canteen strap around his neck and jump to his feet.

If the trail through the woods lasted long enough, Yann believed he would have time to finish the rope. The trail was reasonably easy to walk compared to what he had already traveled. When his hands were free, he needed a place to run to. He had the perfect plan in mind—he needed to find a clearing that would lead to a ledge with a river below; it was the perfect escape, but what was the likelihood of finding that perfect scenario. Instead of dwelling on what might not become a reality, he set his mind on cutting the rope and not his hand like he had done twice already.

The words that Will had spoken to Yann came to mind again—*If you will give the Lord half a chance, He will more than prove Himself to you, that He is who He says He is.* Yann decided to test Will's words. He looked up to the treetops and whispered, "I will give You time to prove Yourself. Show me, Jesus. If You are the one true God that I should worship, make it very clear to me."

It wasn't long after his prayer that the rope fell away from his right hand. *Finally*, he said to himself as he started working on the rope on his left hand. Then, for no apparent reason, Seen slowed to a more comfortable pace that took some of the tension off the rope, making cutting faster and less difficult. He held tight to the rope with his left hand so that Seen wouldn't become suspicious, and then he cut as if his life depended on it, which it did.

Yann could see up ahead that the trail opened up. He hoped it would lead downhill, which might slow Seen down enough to allow him to escape. As the sharp stone made another pass through the heavy leather braided rope, the last bit gave way, freeing him to run. He held tight to the rope and waited patiently for the right moment.

In his heart hope and fear started to war against each other. If he failed Seen would surely make him pay a heavy price for the attempted escape. But he had nothing to lose—death at the hands of his own people or freedom. As they approached the clearing, Yann dropped the rope and ran with all the strength he could muster. His legs were weak and felt like they belonged to someone else—they wouldn't obey his command. He needed to run like a deer and be free.

The clearing pitched downhill, some to the right, but not like he had hoped. It was basically free of trees and rocks, which made it easy to run on but also safe to run a horse over. It took Seen only a moment to ride after him. He stopped his horse a short distance from Yann and jumped down.

His anger had turned to rage. With a red face and the veins swelling in his neck, he moved into a fighting position. "You dog, I should kill you for this! I don't like to be tricked. I never imagined that you would cut my rope." Yann prepared himself for the worst as Seen moved to his left and right. He was yelling more insults and obscenities. Suddenly large beads of sweat appeared on his skin, wetting his clothes, and he started to kick and beat the air as if fighting an invisible enemy, perhaps his own demons from within.

"I'm going to kill you …"

To Yann's astonishment, Seen abruptly stopped and put a hand to his chest and one to his throat. He staggered forward then backward and in circles like a dizzy drunk, moaning and groaning words that Yann couldn't understand because they weren't words, just babblings. He once again stopped and stood still, but this time Seen struggled to breathe. He sounded like he was choking, and then he fell forward and landed on his left side, motionless, as if dead.

Yann stood still as if he were a statue. *Is this a ploy?* he thought. *Is he hoping I will move within range of a hand or foot so that he can catch me off guard?* He quickly moved backward and stood staring at Seen's lifeless body.

As he stood out in the open away from the canopy of the trees, he felt the intensity of the sun. He thought of his canteen and the strap around his neck, and he took a quick drink. The food in Seen's saddlebags came to mind. He was more than just hungry; he was dizzy from the lack of it. The mount that Seen had been riding had wandered off. Yet he dared not leave to search for it, so he backed up into the semi shade and sat down, keeping a close eye on Seen.

After what seemed to be a short eternity of watching Seen's lifeless body, he walked out of the clearing into the woods, but he found no sign of the mount anywhere. He then turned and headed back to the clearing. Once there he saw the second horse eating grass a few feet away from Seen. Yann picked up two stones and tossed them at Seen, but Seen remained motionless. Yann still had his doubts.

He was troubled; he thought he'd be elated with what appeared to be freedom, to be rid of persecutors, but he wasn't. His heart still felt the pain of being a Chinese man in a land that barely tolerated his kind. In addition, he currently did not have any money, equipment, or food. He didn't have a solution to his dilemma.

Suddenly he heard a horse snort, which startled him out of his deep thoughts. He stood to his feet to see a stranger riding up the hill with Seen's horse. The stranger rode toward Yann.

"Did you lose your horse?" the stranger asked.

"Yes, I did."

The man then looked toward where Yann's gaze had traveled. "Young man, is the man lying on the ground dead? And if so, did he die of natural causes or did you kill him?"

"No! I didn't kill him! He tried to kill me, but as he was trying to attack, he grabbed his chest and throat and fell over. He hasn't moved since. I think he's dead, but I'm not sure." The stranger climbed down out of his saddle and handed the reins of Seen's horse to Yann.

"Don't you think it would be wise to check and see if he is dead?"

"I was afraid to. He could be trying to trick me," Yann replied.

The stranger walked over to Seen's body, knelt down, and rolled the body over. He put his ear to his chest, then stood up saying, "He's very dead. He won't be trying to kill you anymore."

Yann took a deep breath and slowly exhaled. Long held emotions rolled over him that he couldn't put into words. He turned away and opened the saddlebags, hoping to find something to eat. He removed what he found and placed his nose in the middle of it, just for the smell.

"I think we should bury him. The animals will be after him if we don't," commented the stranger.

With bread in one hand, cheese in the other, and a mouthful of both, Yann just nodded his head yes.

"You look tired and hungry. Why don't you sit down and eat. I'll dig the hole."

"Thanks," Yann said.

"I have a shovel with me," the stranger mentioned.

Yann sat down and watched as the stranger dug the hole. The man was more than six feet tall. He had the look of a man of years though he moved like a young man full of energy and strength. He was different, unique.

"What's your name?" Yann asked.

He looked over with a smile and said, "I'm Samuel. Who do you claim to be?"

"I'm Yann Chang, and I have a second question for you. How old are you?"

"My age isn't important, but trust me, I'm plenty old. I suppose you want to know where I'm from, right? Well, the answer to that is the East," Samuel said as he continued to dig.

"I thought it might be the Northwest by the way you're dressed," Yann commented.

Samuel climbed out of the hole and said, "There, it's finished. Now let's take care of this poor soul."

Yann stood up and looked at the grave. Then he looked Samuel in the eyes and said, "How did you dig that grave so quickly?"

"It wasn't difficult," Samuel answered.

They both took hold of an arm and leg and carefully lowered Seen into his resting place. Samuel handed Yann the shovel and said, "Why don't you cover him, and I'll start collecting rocks." Yann wasted no time filling in the grave. As he worked, he was overcome with a strange kind of peace, a sense of satisfaction.

Samuel returned with the first armload of rocks and dropped them by the grave and went back for another. Yann took this as a sign that the covering of rocks was also his responsibility. Samuel returned and dropped the last of the rocks at his feet. Yann finished filling in the grave. Before placing the last rock at its resting place, he said aloud, "Seen, this is my rock of freedom."

"Yann, are you headed any place in particular?" Samuel asked from the saddle.

"Yes, north to Fort Reading to meet up with friends. Why? Are you thinking of riding with me?"

"I can ride to the fort with you, then I'm headed south. You are taking both of the gentleman's horses aren't you? They look like fine animals," stated Samuel.

Yann looked at him a little funny and said, "Gentleman! You have such respect, even for a man like him that you never knew." He took another piece of bread from the saddlebag, then mounted and rode toward the trail through the woods. After a time Samuel rode up beside him and handed him something wrapped in cheesecloth.

"What's this?"

"Food. I believe you're still hungry," Samuel said.

Yann quickly unwrapped it to find a bread and butter sandwich with a thickly cut piece of fish lying neatly between the two slices of bread. "Where did you get this? It looks like it's fresh," Yann said just before he took a large bite out of it.

"It was extra, that's all, and I'm not going to need it," he said with a slight smile.

Yann led the way. He ate slowly, enjoying every bite of his sandwich. They left the shaded trail, passed by the dry stream bed where Yann had laid face down in, then down the ridge west to the main wagon road.

Yann was filled with amazement at what had taken place. Seen was dead and buried, Mui was nowhere in sight, and now he was riding the horse of the one who had hunted him. *In China, to ride your enemy's horse would bring great honor*, he mused.

Samuel, a man younger than his years, had shown up at the most needed time with help, strength, and food. And not just any trail food, but fresh food. When he finished the sandwich, Samuel handed him a peach and said, "I think you'll like this. It's an extra, too."

Samuel rode up in front of Yann. "We're going to need to camp for the night. There should be a comfortable place to stop up ahead. It will be dusk soon."

Yann followed Samuel off the road through a stand of cedar trees that filled his nostrils with their strong scent. They weaved their way through a maze of trees and dodged branches for about fifty yards on a poorly marked path, but they suddenly emerged into a small clearing with a fire pit in the center that was encircled with fist-sized rocks.

"This is where I'd like to lay my head for the night. It looks comfortable," Samuel said with a look of accomplishment on his face.

"How did you know that this place was here, Samuel, seeing that it was hidden so well by the trees?"

"A friend told me about it, and I'm blessed with a good sense of direction, so it wasn't hard to find."

They both dismounted and tied their horses to a tree that just happened to have grass growing at its base. Yann stripped the saddles and bits from the horses and sat down by the fire pit. The sound of water caught his attention, but he didn't move because it felt good to sit and relax.

"I'll make you a deal, Yann Chang."

"What's that?"

"If you'll fill the canteens, I'll start the fire. What do you say to that?"

"That's fair. Hand me your canteen, and I'll do it."

He headed off in the direction of the sound of the water. He found a brook not far from the clearing. It was sweet and cold. He filled the canteens and took a long drink before rinsing his face and wetting his hair. His mind traveled back to China and images of the days when he would go to the bathhouse in his home village. After his bath he would go and see Sanne to talk and dream of their future. How enjoyable it would be to hear her voice once more.

Samuel was squatting by the fire adding wood when Yann returned.

"Nice fire," Yann said.

"What do you think about beans and leftover bread?"

"Do I have a choice, Samuel?"

"Yes, you always have a choice. You just have to make the right one, that's all."

"Beans and bread it is then."

Yann sat down and leaned against his saddle and folded his arms. He closed his eyes and let his mind focus once again on Sanne. He loved her very much, and he didn't want to spend the rest of his life without her.

Now that he was no longer hunted, he must formulate a plan to bring her to America. That would be a challenge, and he knew that. His people could help in getting word back to her family to send her to him. That was a beginning.

"As the beans cook, tell me why the man was trying to kill you?" Samuel's question roused Yann from his planning.

"It started in China. The governor of my province accused me of being part of a political takeover and attempted murder of him and his family. I had no part in it, but they do not, and will not, believe that I'm innocent. They sent Seen and a second man to bring me back so they could remove my head. This has torn my heart out and separated me from my future bride and family, from everything I know. It has brought me to a land where the Chinese are hated. We have little or no rights as a people here in America. Samuel, I'm tired of explaining this. It haunts me. It hovers over me like a thick black cloud. I need help from my people."

"I can see that you need a lot of help, but help has already been provided. Do you see it, Yann?"

"Well, yes, in the way that you showed up. You gave me food; you dug the grave; you've been a great help. Thank you for that."

"The help I've given is very little. Look at the grand picture of your life, Yann. You're here and not in China, the governor's hand can no longer reach you. Think of Seen and the other man. You're free from their powers. And about Sanne, be patient and trust, and you will have the desires of your heart."

"Tell me, who are you?"

"I'm Samuel, just like I said, and I was asked to help you. That's all, nothing more and nothing less. Is that strange to you—that I would come along at the right time and give you a helping hand? I receive great satisfaction from doing things for others, don't you?"

"Yes, sometimes, but what do you mean that you were asked to give me a hand? Who asked you?" Yann asked with interest.

"The Lord asked me to help you. Haven't you heard Him speak to you before?"

"I don't know if I have. I've talked to God before, and listened, but I'm confused. It's like what I told Will. I was raised with two different beliefs and it's hard to see things clearly. Samuel, how can you be so confident about what you believe?"

"It's in the heart. The way He loves me; the way He speaks to me. He guides me. He's always with me and that gives me peace. He only wants the best for us. This morning I asked, 'What would you like me to do today, Lord,' and He led me to you."

"When I stop and think about it, I did ask for help today. I prayed and asked God to show Himself to me," Yann said.

"What was your answer?" Samuel leaned forward in anticipation.

"Well, things happened. I cut the rope and started to escape, but Seen came after me in a rage, yelling, swearing, threatening to kill me. He climbed down off his horse and moved toward me, but then he started acting strangely, and before I knew it he had fallen over and died."

"I see that you still don't understand. What you just explained to me sounds like your prayer was answered, or at least in part. The Lord works that way sometimes. He'll answer us step by step as we learn to follow Him."

"How did you get your hands on the stone to cut the rope, my friend?"

"When I fell in the dry wash, it ended up in my hand."

"That was very convenient, wouldn't you say, Yann?"

"Do you think that God gave me the stone, helped me cut the rope, and killed Seen to help me escape?"

"I'm going to answer your question in an indirect way. I do think that life is a matter of choices, and we have two roads to choose from: one of evil and one of good. It sounds like Seen chose the evil one. Now, as far as the stone and the escape is concerned, the Lord has quietly and invisibly done many things for many people throughout history. In the Bible Peter and Paul were freed more than once, and God is the same God today."

"When it comes to God, I become confused. I can't see my way through it. I want peace and I want to trust."

"What is it that's stopping you from having that?"

"What if I follow Christ but it's Buddha that I should be following?"

"That's a fair question to be asking. My Bible is in my saddlebag. Let me read something to you. I think it will help. Why don't you start eating while you listen. The beans are more than done by now."

Samuel retrieved his Bible and sat down, leaning against his saddle near the firelight, for the sun was completely down by now.

"This is from the book of Matthew, 'Ask, and it will be given to you; seek and you will find; knock and the door will be opened to you. For everyone who asks receives; the one who seeks finds; and to the one who knocks, the door will be opened. Which of you, if your son asks for bread, will give him a stone? Or if he asks for a fish, will give him a snake? If you, then, though you are evil, know how to give good gifts to your children, how much more will your Father in heaven give good things to those who ask him!'"

"My father read that to me years ago. He is a believer in Christ."

"Then ask, Yann, just like it says here. Ask, and it will be given to you. Then watch and see what happens. Look at what has already happened!"

Samuel flipped through the pages of his Bible and then stopped. "This is from the book of Mark, and it's very plain what the Lord is telling us both: 'Therefore I tell you, whatever you ask for in prayer, believe that you have received it, and it will be yours.'"

"Samuel, I hear all of what you are saying, but in my heart I don't feel that trust that I see or hear in others. I have such doubt inside."

They both sat quietly for a few moments before Samuel said, "Try to picture this, Yann. You made a bad choice and ended up in a desperate situation. To your back is a ravine a thousand feet down and a solid stone wall in front of you that is also impossible to climb. The narrow path you've been on ends where you're standing. You can't go back because the log that you crossed on broke in two just as you stepped on the other side, which left you no way to return.

"You have enough food and water for one day, but you didn't bring a rope or any other equipment with you. Now time has passed and all food and water is gone. The weather is turning bad, and you have given up hope of ever getting out alive.

"Then you see a man walking toward you on the path. He says, 'I followed your tracks here because I know from experience that this path can be deadly. I also know that you're hungry and tired, so I'll help you across the ravine to safety.' You're amazed that he's come to help and you ask, 'Tell me, how can you help?' The man smiles and says, 'Just trust me.'

"You both make your way back to the edge of the ravine and you find that he has cut a log and laid it across the hollow. The man then says, 'Yes, I cut it for you, and you're going first so I can steady you from behind.' Yann, you make it to the other side safely, but the log snaps in two, and the man falls to his death at the bottom of the ravine. This leaves you standing in silent horror that this man died so you could live.

"How would that affect you? Would you quickly forget and go your way or would this life-saving experience be etched in your mind forever?"

Samuel spooned himself some food as Yann put down his plate and said, "I understand what you're trying to do, but I don't know just what I think about all of this. In my mind things become like a bowl of noodle soup, all mixed up and confused. I suppose I need time or something to sort it out."

"Every man has to be convinced in his own heart about the things of God, and it does take time, for some men more and others less, but every man needs time, and you are no exception," stated Samuel.

"Time heals, that I know. By the way, this cut on my cheek needs to heal, also. Do you have any salve? It is becoming very sore, and I think it my be infected."

"Yes, I do. It's in my medicine bag. Did Seen do that to you?"

"Not directly. When I fell in the wash, my face hit a sharp rock. The cut is making my face ache."

"This salve will help. It has a lot of good things in it. An Indian friend gave it to me."

"When was that, Samuel?"

"Oh ... thousands of years ago. This salve is as old as the hills," he said with a laugh.

"Samuel, how long are you going to ride with me?"

"I told you until we reach Fort Reading where your friends are."

"They reached the fort days ago and have left by now. I told Will not to wait for me if we were ever separated, that he should continue on and find his wife."

"The Lord told me that you'll meet up with them soon."

"Sometimes you seem to be more than a man, Samuel. You're hard to understand."

"I'm a servant of God, just like you can be if you choose to," Samuel said.

"Yes, if I choose to, and if I don't?"

"Then you're in danger of becoming an enemy of God, because any man who is a friend of this world is an enemy of God. No one can have it both ways—you cannot serve two masters. But you're not an enemy of God, Yann. You just haven't decided who to serve, that's all."

"There is hope then? I've been anxious for a long time now due to my confusion."

"God is more longsuffering than you think. He loves you very much and wants you to be in paradise with Him."

"I would like to be in paradise," he said thoughtfully.

"What about Sanne? Does she believe in Christ?"

A smile came across Yann's face as he said, "She's beautiful, delicate, and an artist. She paints and makes pottery with her mother and father. We love each other very much, and I want us to marry, but how will I marry her now? I am here, and she is there. That makes me very angry!"

"Anger can be good if it's used in the right way—use your anger to do good and not evil. Could Sanne's father, with the help of your father, send her to San Francisco like they did you?" Samuel asked.

Yann sat up and said, "Before we began to eat, I was resting and wondering if it would be possible for Sanne to come to America. But I just don't know if that is possible. You make it sound so simple."

"Maybe you were too angry to think or see clearly," Samuel stated.

"You could be right. At times I get beside myself as you Americans say."

"Yann, I want to ask the Lord to make it possible for you to see and believe. Can I pray for you?"

Yann hesitated and then said, "All right, go ahead and pray."

"Holy Father, I thank you for loving us the way You do and for giving us Jesus. For in Him dwells all the fullness of the Godhead bodily, and we are complete in Him, who is the head of all principality and power. Lord, I ask that You will bless Yann and Sanne. Please bring them back together so they can be husband and wife. Please protect her from danger, Lord.

"I know You have many ways that I know nothing about, Holy Father, and I ask that You surprise us with some of them. Father, I ask this in faith. Please teach Yann Your will for his life that he may have faith and believe. Thank you, Father, in Jesus' most powerful name, amen."

Yann said nothing—he just stared up at the night sky. He didn't answer the question about Sanne's belief in Christ, because in his heart he didn't actually know. He loved her so much that he was afraid to ask her at the beginning of their relationship.

"The stars are wonderful, aren't they?" Samuel asked.

"Yes, I enjoy them. I've asked before if there's an end to it all, and no one has ever given me an answer."

"I don't think there is an end to the heavens. Everywhere I look there are stars."

"I don't know what to think," Yann said.

"Do you think that the One who created the stars and guides their paths can direct your life?"

Yann heard Samuel's question, but he acted like he didn't. His mind was dwelling on the story of the man, the path, and the log. He understood the man to be Christ, the path as his decisions in life, and the log to be the cross of Christ. If Christ had truly died to save him and the Bible was true, Yann knew he could believe.

"Samuel, I've been thinking about the story you told me, and I think I understand how big of a sacrifice Christ gave for us. But how do I win over this doubt that I have?"

"You must choose to believe, Yann! What you've been told, believe it to be true and stop all this doubting. Do you remember what I read a few minutes ago? When you ask, believe that you will receive, and you shall have it. Just choose to believe!"

Yann repeated again and again in his head, *Just choose to believe.*

"Yann, eat this last piece of bread before it becomes as hard as a rock."

"Do you have a family, Samuel?"

"No I don't; I never married. We all have different gifts, different callings. You could say I have a very large family with many children because I have brothers and sisters who have children, and I have a lot of friends.

"As for your calling, Yann, I believe in time that you and Sanne will be together."

"I hope you're right."

"Choose to believe without doubting," Samuel repeated.

"That's not always easy to do," Yann stated as he yawned. "I need some sleep. I feel drained."

"I would think so. With a weary body and a full stomach, you should sleep like a bear. I'll clean the pot or the animals will pay us a visit tonight," Samuel said as he jumped up and headed for the stream by the light of a partial moon.

At the edge of the stream he filled the pot with water, then he knelt down and prayed, "Holy Father, please send Your Spirit to Yann's heart so he can see that You are the only wise, true, and living God and Jesus Christ whom You have sent. I pray that the doubt in him can be driven away, that Satan can be driven away, so he can believe. Dear Father, I want Jesus to be glorified in Yann, that You, Father, can be glorified in Jesus. Please be with Sanne. Protect her and bring them together. Holy Father, I thank you and ask this in Jesus' all-powerful name, amen."

Samuel stood to his feet and looked straight up to the sky and said, "Thank you, Father, for hearing me." He then washed the pot and went back to camp where he quickly fell asleep with joy and peace in his heart.

෴෴෴෴෴

Yann opened his eyes to find Samuel cooking. "How long have you been up? You're as quiet as a deer eating from a fall garden."

"I'm going to take that as a compliment, Yann. Come and eat my corn cakes while they're hot."

"May I ask how you made them here?"

"There's no time for cooking lessons today, Yann. I know you're anxious to catch up with your friends, so let's get going!"

It wasn't long before they were packed and on horseback. They had talked so much the night before that it seemed only right to ride hard and in silence.

"Yann," said Samuel, intruding on his thoughts, "we've made good time. We should see Nobles Trail in about an hour which will leave you plenty of daylight to continue on."

"True, but time passes like a bird in flight very quickly. The ride is going to be dangerous for me, a Chinese man traveling alone with a good horse and gear. Someone could accuse me of stealing it and take it from me and then put me in jail. I wish you were riding with me until I meet up with them. I would feel better about it."

"Yann, I have prayed for you. Remember, choose to believe. The Lord is with you, and so are His angels. They will protect you, and you will safely meet up with your friends."

The wagon road grew steeper on the approach to Nobles Trail where Fort Reading sat. Yann could feel the stress build in his chest as the time drew near when he would ride alone. In the space of roughly forty-eight hours, he had become comfortable and at peace riding with Samuel, and he wished it wouldn't end.

"My friend, this is where we part. The Lord will direct you. Be at peace, and remember, the Lord only desires to do good to you."

"Thank you for all the help. You've done more for me than I probably realize, and you won't be easily forgotten." Yann stretched out his arm and shook Samuel's hand. "Take care."

"And likewise to you, my friend," said Samuel.

They released hands and rode off in different directions.

❧❧❧❧❧

Will looked up at the sign above the door. It read W. J. Woodfield Mercantile, *If We Don't Have It, They Don't Make It.* As he entered the store, he found it busy with people. A tall, heavy man behind the counter stood. "What can I do for you?"

"I need some information," Will answered.

"That's the only thing that's free here. I'm W. J., the owner of this establishment," he replied.

"I'm looking for three men and a woman. They're riding north. One tall man and two short men, one drags a spur and his name is Charlie. The woman is twenty-seven and pretty. She's five seven with long brown hair. Have you seen them?"

W. J. hooked his thumbs into the straps of his suspenders and said, "Ya, I did, two days ago. The tall one with the short one came in; it's the short man who drags a spur. I know it's the ones you're looking for because the short one rubbed his hip and made the comment that it was killing him."

At that moment a short thin woman pushed back a curtain behind the counter and stepped out. "I overheard you two, and I have a few things to add. The two men bought beans, flour, salt, a plug of tobacco, and a few other goods. The third man stayed outside with the woman," she said.

Will could hardly contain himself. "How did she look?"

"I didn't see her up close, just through the window from here. She wore a blue calico dress without a bonnet, but her hair was up in a bun."

"The dress had some yellow in it, didn't it?" Will asked.

"Yes, there was yellow in it, now that you mention it," the woman said.

"I bought that dress for her," Will replied.

"Just who are you anyway?" W. J. asked.

"I'm Will Jacobs, the sheriff of Stone Ridge, below Marysville. I've been tracking them for weeks. The woman is my wife, and the men kidnapped her." Will swallowed hard as he said the last sentence.

"Now that I think about it more, it was three days ago, about eleven in the morning. As they started to ride out, I stepped over to the door and watched them. They all rode north out of town. Maybe they're headed for Yreka. They seemed to be in a real hurry, very impatient," the woman added.

"Those men should get a bullet or two each," W. J. said.

"Thanks," said Will, "you've told me plenty."

As he headed for the door, the woman called out, "Sheriff! I hope you find your wife. Best of luck!"

Standing on the boardwalk, he could see Tanger across the street heading in his direction, but with all the noise and commotion, it was useless to try and get his attention. Will maneuvered through the maze of draft animals and wagons to reach him.

As they met, Will said in a loud voice, "They were here three days ago. They rode north toward Yreka."

When they reached their horses, they found themselves penned in, not only by the mounts hitched next to their own but also a wagon full of goods, which was drawn by a team of six mules and had pulled alongside, finishing the blockade.

Tanger looked around and yelled loudly, "Who's the man in charge of this team? Could you move it; you've blocked us in!"

A young man with a scraggly beard and shoulder length hair approached the wagon. He climbed in and drove away without saying a word.

They mounted their horses and were turning to head out of town when Tanger looked down the street in the opposite direction and said with great surprise, "Do you see what I see, Will!"

"No, what do you see?"

"Yann! He's riding down the middle of the street headed our way."

"He's free? Whose horse is he riding?"

"Maybe it's Seen's horse. I guess he solved his problem," Tanger said.

They maneuvered through the crowded street and met Yann in the middle.

"Yann, it's good to see you!" Will said.

Tanger patted Yann on the back as he said, "I missed you, but obviously you made it!"

"What happened to you, Will?" Yann asked.

"I'll tell you later. Emma's been here. We're riding farther north, come on. I'll tell you what happened to me as we ride. It's been quite an adventure," Will said.

"I have much to tell you, too," Yann said excitedly.

Chapter Six

Perfect Timing

"Charlie, will you stop it! All you've done is complain since we got off the Noble Trail. You know I want this job over with just as much as you do. I can't help it if Wyler changed the plans. He doesn't want any trouble with the Modoc. Can you blame him? Do you want to fight the Modoc, Charlie? You know by staying on the wagon road we'll probably all live longer. So tell me what's really bothering you; it can't just be the delay."

"You know I don't like horses that much, and my hip is killing me from all the ridin'. I wanted to keep the wagon, Lester."

"The wagon was too slow; we couldn't keep it."

"That doesn't make me feel any better," Charlie said as he rubbed his hip.

"What is it with your hip, anyway? You've never said."

"What good is talkin' about it going to do?"

"Maybe you'll stop complaining about it if you let it out," Lester said.

"All right, for what it's worth, when I was a kid a friend of mine who lived down the road and I were playing at his place when his horse reared up and knocked me down and then stepped on me. I've never walked right since, and the older I get, the worse it gets. I suppose the day is comin' when I won't get around much at all, then how am I gonna earn a living? I'm fortunate I'm not a drunk by now with this pain."

"You'll have to change your ways, I guess. I know you live in pain, but there's something more on your mind than that."

"I'm afraid, Lester!"

"Afraid? Afraid of what? I've never seen you afraid before."

"This job is different. We've robbed, rustled cattle, beat a few men and more, but we've never kidnapped anyone, and to top it off, a lawman's wife. We could hang for this, Lester. I think we've gone too far this time. I should have said no and went panning for gold."

"All the easy gold is gone, and you know it, Charlie. We did take a big chance with the woman, but it also pays big, and that's why you agreed, so stop the fussing!"

"Lester, if her man is a fast gun, we're in trouble, and he may not be ridin' alone. Did you ever think of that?"

"Yes, I've thought about it a lot. We have to take the good with the bad; that's the way it is!"

Charlie twisted in his saddle and looked behind him to see how far Joey and the woman were lagging behind. "I've got to rest my hip and get off this horse; the pain is almost too much for me."

"Charlie, we've only got another day's ride, can you make it that far?"

"Yeah, but I need some rest."

"Joey, we're stopping here! I want the woman to sit next to me," Lester said. They dismounted and Charlie stretched out on the ground, giving him some relief. He closed his eyes and tried to relax.

"Let me know when you're ready to ride, Charlie. Woman, I want you to start planning the food for supper. There are plenty of supplies," Lester told her.

Being the only woman, it was natural for the men to take advantage of her cooking skills, but as long as she put them into practice she ate well too.

She was thankful for the way the Lord was speaking to her heart through this whole ordeal. She was not to complain or cause trouble, and most of all, she was not to run away. Joseph, a man of faith, was the Bible character who the Lord showed Emma she was to emulate. The Lord was with Joseph, and he was a successful man. The Lord made all he did prosper. From his days of slavery to his leadership as prime minister, the Lord had been with him and blessed him. Man had intended evil against him, but the Lord brought good out of evil. She was asked to show the same spirit as Joseph, which is also the spirit of Christ.

Even in her situation she still had things to be thankful for. Lester had some degree of trust in her—he never did tie her up at night as he said he would. And as of yet, she still hadn't been beaten or wrongly touched. The Lord was protecting her. There were a few things she would deeply appreciate though—a hot bath, a change of clothes, and a bed to sleep in—but for now the Lord had withheld them from her.

The thought of her past came to mind. Had she put herself in this position? The Bible says that your sins will surely seek you out and find you. Had the results of her past life finally found her and were demanding payment? Emma knew she was forgiven for her past, but sometimes that doesn't erase the effects of the past.

At fifteen she had run away from a very abusive and broken home. Her parents had thought it better to take care of their own needs and pleasures than the needs of their little girl who they brought into the world. Emma was a product of her environment: undisciplined, selfish, insecure, and very needy. In her young and inexperienced eyes, running away with an older man seemed wise—what followed was neither constructive nor peaceful. It was a painful thought to remember, and it brought tears to her eyes that spilled out and ran down her cheeks.

"Now what are you crying about, woman?" Lester said harshly. His demanding voice made her flinch.

"Are you thinking about your man and how he's going to rescue your poor soul? Is he going to be a hero, woman?"

The temptation was strong to blurt out the words, "Yes, he is going to rescue me, and when he does, all of you will be sorry because he's a faithful man and he loves me and I'm important to him." She also wanted to add that they couldn't stop him because God was with him, but she didn't. She bit her tongue. The stress had affected her stomach days ago, but this incident just made the knot tighter.

"Let's go," Lester yelled at Charlie.

"I'll give it a try," Charlie said as he struggled to his feet and moved slowly toward his horse.

"You heard me, let's go." It made Lester feel important to have the last word.

The others sat mounted as Charlie took his time getting in the saddle. Once mounted, he looked over and said, "One of you could have helped me up ya know."

"You didn't ask!" Lester said.

"You guys don't like each others, do ya?"

"What was that, Joey?" Lester asked.

"Nothin', I didn't say nothin'."

The trail got tougher heading out of Yreka as it made its way up through the Sierra Nevada mountain range. The harder trail slowed their pace considerably, which was the last thing they wanted. The trails at times were busy with more of the same, emigrants and mule-drawn supply wagons with narrow spots along the way. No one said much because there wasn't much to say; the goal was to just ride, ride, and ride. After riding for another extended period of time, Charlie saw a good place to stop up ahead on the left that featured a flat area with trees in the background. When they reached the area Charlie pulled off and stopped.

"Not another rest, Charlie!" Lester protested.

"Just a short one, I promise. I'm getting cramps down my right leg," he stated.

They all dismounted and found a resting place, all expect Charlie. He walked in small circles, rubbing his leg, trying to work the cramps out. "Let me sit for a few minutes, then we'll go."

He squatted to sit down, and at that very moment he felt a sharp pain and a popping sound in his right hip, causing him to fall to the ground and grab his hip. He had never felt such pain, and to add to the experience, there was a new round of cramps. "Aahhhhh! My hip! I can't take the pain! I can't ride anymore!" he cried out.

He rolled over on his back and tried with great effort to straighten out his leg, but this created so much more pain that beads of sweat appeared on his face.

"What happened?"

"I don't know what's wrong, but I'm not goin' anywhere!"

"Charlie, you know if you can't make it the rest of the way you'll have to stay behind and catch up with me later."

"What kind of a partner are you? Just as soon as I'm down, you leave me dry. You can't be trusted. The next thing you'll do is run off with all the money." In spite of the pain Charlie felt, he tried to draw his gun on Lester. But before he could clear his holster, Lester had drawn and cocked his pistol.

"If you ever pull a gun on me again, I'll shoot you. Do you understand, Charlie? Now toss your gun to me!" Lester said, keeping his gun steadied on him.

"As I said, you can catch up with me at the cabin. I'm going to leave you the axe, some food, and the rope. Joey is staying with you. You'll need his help, and he can build one of those Indian things like a stretcher that you pull behind the horse if you can't ride. I saw one once. It has long arms that tie to the back of the horse. Do you know what I'm talking about, Joey?"

"Yeah, I can make one," Joey said.

"Then start making one. Charlie, you're going to get paid, but not until this job is done. Here, take the note with the directions. I can find my way," Lester said with a look of disappointment on his face.

"Woman, get on your horse, and let's go." Lester walked his horse a distance from Charlie and hung the gun on a branch. He turned and said to Charlie, "This will give me time to ride off without having to watch my backside." He mounted and they rode off quickly.

Charlie stayed lying on his back, and through the pain he stewed over horses and how they had messed up the majority of his life. He also stewed about a partner who he could no longer trust and the dull-witted Joey who he was stuck with. Could things get much worse?

"Joey, how long is this going to take you?"

"I just started. I'm trying to do it fast," he said as he swung the axe into the tree.

Joey cut down three trees. The first two were approximately sixteen feet long and the third around ten feet. He then trimmed all the branches off the three. The third and shortest of the three was then cut into two separate pieces, each about three feet long. He proceeded to build the stretcher frame using the rope to hold it together. Then, taking one of the bedrolls, he cut a strip of blanket a foot wide, which was the length of the blanket, and he attached it to one end of the frame for support and strength.

85

The strip of blanket and poles were then attached to the back of the horse just behind the saddle and to the saddle. The rest of the blanket was pulled tight over the frame for Charlie to lie down on. All of this took about an hour of their time. Charlie silently hoped the frame was secure enough to hold his not so thin body. Joey finished attaching it to Charlie's mount and then pulled the horse alongside him.

"Now, Charlie, I've got to get you on this thing." He bent over and took Charlie by the shoulders and lifted his top half onto the stretcher and then his legs.

"I didn't think you could do it," Charlie admitted. "And it's reasonably comfortable, too."

Joey nodded his head in agreement, mounted his horse, and rode off with Charlie in tow.

Charlie found it impossible to sleep or rest because of the pain, along with the noise of the stretcher being drug over the ground, so he pulled the note from his right pants pocket to try to pass some time. Unfolding it he read, "Lester, there's a change in plans. Do not take the Nobles to Goose Lake; the Modoc are making trouble. Turn around and head for Yreka. Take the wagon road about fifteen miles out. On the right side of the trail, you'll see a horse path with two piles of rocks on the left side of the path—take that three-quarters of a mile, and you'll come to cabin. I'll meet you, the woman, and Charlie there, Wyler."

"We should be there pretty soon. It's only fifteen miles out of Yreka. Lester acted like it was a two-day ride for crying out loud. Look for a horse path on the right with two piles of rocks on the left side of the path. Take that horse path to the cabin. Did you hear me, Joey?"

"Yeah, I heard ya! Are we gonna stay there for a while?"

"Yes, and we're meeting up with Wyler. Then we get paid for all of this hard work," Charlie said with a bit of satisfaction.

"Who's Wyler, Charlie?"

"The boss of this job!"

"I thought Lester was the boss, Charlie."

"He's not, and never mind the rest!" he said, shaking his head.

Joey started thinking about all that he and Emma had told each other. He thought she was really nice. She treated him kindly, and she talked a lot about

Jesus and how He loves everyone. They had become friends, and he trusted her. He had learned the hard way that Lester wasn't trustworthy.

He wished things were different and that he hadn't helped them kidnap her. He knew he was in serious trouble and that it might be too late now. Lester had lied to him from the beginning; he was told that he had a job that would pay more than he had ever been paid before. The job was working with horses, which he loved, but he didn't like hurting Emma.

His conscience troubled him, but he didn't know what do about the situation. Lester might shoot him if he tried to help Emma escape, and what good would that do. He needed to talk to her. *She's smart; she'll know what to do,* he thought. He picked up the pace toward the cabin, feeling a little better about his decision.

"Say, Joey, what are you going to do with your part of the money?"

"I don't know, my ma and pa are dead, and my big brother don't care for me. He says I'm stupid just because I'm no good at reading and all. I don't know where I'm goin' when all this is done."

"You're good with horses and building things—you did a good job with this stretcher. Why don't you stay here in California? And by the way, you're not stupid. I wasn't that good at school, either. I can read all right, but I'm not good with numbers."

"You need my help, don't ya, Charlie. That's why you're treatin' me nice, because you can't ride. I know I'm right, Charlie."

"I need your help all right. I can't ride, and I don't know if I can even walk again!"

"I don't trust you, Charlie, just like I don't trust Lester. He lied to me about this job. He said I was gonna work with horses and he would pay me real good. Tell me, Charlie, why are we hurting Emma and her little girl? I've watched her, and she treats us nice. Even when you and Lester are mean to her, she treats you nice."

"That just goes along with the job. I don't even think about it; I guess I'm just mean-spirited. I've been this way most of my life, and I can't see myself changing. You said you can't trust me, and I know trust has to be earned, but once I get my money you'll never see me again. So there's no need to worry about trusting me, is there?"

Joey didn't respond to Charlie. He didn't know what to say.

"Are you done talking, Joey?"

"I don't know what to say, but I heard what you said, Charlie."

"I need it quiet anyway, just keep lookin' for the rocks on the path."

The talking had helped him keep his mind off the pain, which he still had plenty of, but he didn't like talking about feelings and life, so he retreated back to his own thoughts. He was now realizing that the fifteen miles to the cabin was wrong. He was hoping to beat the darkness, but if not, there was the light from the three-quarter moon. *If only I had some laudanum,* he thought, *it would deaden the pain or almost take it away.*

After crossing the Klamath River, the wagon traffic slowed down. Most of the emigrants pulled off the trail for the night so both man and beast could rest. He was still holding out hope that some passerby would have a swallow or two of laudanum.

Not more than a minute or two later Charlie heard what sounded like an empty buckboard hitting potholes and bumps along the way. "Is that a buckboard coming?"

"Yeah, it is," Joey said.

"Stop when you reach it."

When Joey approached the buckboard, he stopped to his right. The old man pulled back on the reins and came to a full stop. He was definitely an old timer, maybe seventy or so, with little or no hair left on his head. It seemed that all of his energy went into growing his beard, which was fully white, thick, and nearly touched his belt around his waist. His coat looked oversized on his thin frame.

"It looks like you ran into some trouble. Did ya break a leg?" the old man asked

"No, I've got a bad hip and can't ride. Would you have some laudanum to help me with the pain, old timer?"

"I'm Ned, what's your name?"

"Charlie, do ya have some?" he asked with hope

Ned reached into his left coat pocket and pulled out an almost full bottle of laudanum. He held up the bottle, showing the reason for having it—a hand full of deformed fingers nearly bent off at a right angle due to rheumatism.

"I would think this is what you're lookin' for."

"Ya, I'll take it." Charlie reached for it.

Ned pulled back his hand and said, "Not so fast; I want a twenty dollar gold piece." He held out his other hand for payment.

"Twenty dollars!"

"It's gonna cost you that much in Yreka, and how much pain are you in?" Ned replied with a large smile, showing off his crooked and partially rotten teeth.

Charlie pushed his hand into his pants pocket and pulled out a twenty dollar gold piece. He wasn't aware that at the same time the note came out with it and tumbled to the ground. Charlie pressed the gold piece into the palm of the old timers hand and quickly took hold of the bottle. He removed the cork and took a swallow.

"Joey, let's be on our way. Thank you for the laudanum, old timer."

As the two rode away, the old timer yelled, "My name is Ned!"

Ned stared at the retreating forms as they traveled down the road and out of sight. As he turned to slap the reins and continue on his way, he noticed something out of the corner of his eye. It was a piece of paper lying on the ground. He climbed down, picked it up, and quickly placed it in his coat pocket. He then climbed back into the buckboard and laughed a childlike laugh, excited about finding the note. He fantasized about its contents as he went on his way.

The laudanum quickly began doing its job. Charlie's pain was no longer demanding first place in his mind, and his anger toward Lester over the money seemed to slide off into the distance. Things were rather pleasant now—he was at peace. It's amazing what a tincture of opium will do. It created a false sense of security for him. His life still had the dark cloud hanging over it, but he just couldn't see it in his drug-induced state.

Charlie fell asleep, and faithful to his word, Joey carefully watched for the path, which he spotted ahead in the distance. Dusk was on the way and the note proved to be true—two piles of stones stood on the left side of the path. Joey turned toward it and said in a loud voice, "Charlie, here's the path. This won't take long."

Charlie heard the voice but it sounded far off. He raised his head and could see the path and the two piles of stones. "I must have fallen asleep; that laudanum's strong stuff." *Three-quarters of a mile and we're at the cabin*, he thought to himself.

Lester heard someone coming and stepped to the door of the cabin. He put his hand to his pistol as a precaution, and Emma peeked from the corner of the window. He could hear the horses along with a dragging sound, which alerted him to the fact that it was Joey and Charlie. Then Joey appeared in the clearing with his goods in tow. He pulled up to the front of the cabin, stopped, and dismounted.

"Congratulations! You made better time than I thought you would," Lester said.

"It was farther than you thought it was," Charlie stated. "Did Wyler make it?"

"He hasn't shown up yet, so we have to sit and wait," Lester stated.

"And what if he doesn't show, then what? We're stuck holding the woman!" Charlie said with some concern.

"He'll be here, probably tomorrow. He wants the woman, like I said before. Wyler has some kind of a connection to her. We just don't know what it is," Lester said.

"I don't know who Wyler is. I honestly don't understand what he wants from me," Emma said fearfully.

"I wasn't askin' your opinion, woman. You'll find out soon enough right along with the rest of us."

"Is there any food for us to eat, Lester?"

"There's food around the corner of the cabin. Tie the horses in the trees with the others."

Joey led the horses and Charlie away. He unhooked the stretcher, placed him flat on the ground, and walked away with the horses.

Charlie looked up at the sky and said, "This is not gonna work. Joey, bring my saddle over. I need to sit up. I can't eat this way," he yelled.

Joey could be stubborn. He heard what Charlie had said, but he continued taking care of the horses. *When I'm done Charlie will get his saddle,* he thought.

Emma walked over to Joey and said, "I'm glad you're back. You're the only friend I have here. Can I help you with the horses?"

"No, I can do it. I need to tell you what I'm thinkin' about. I'm gonna help you escape. It's not right that we took you away from your little girl and hurt you, too. Somethin' bad is gonna happen. I can tell we need to get away."

"I can't run away. If I do my husband won't find me, and we could get hurt, or even worse, maybe killed. I don't want that, Joey. I feel impressed from God that it would be best if I waited for my husband, and that's what I'm going to do. I don't want to cause any trouble, Joey. When my husband gets here, I'm going to tell him how much you've helped me and that you've been so kind."

"Lester lied to me. He said it was a horse job, not a kidnapping job. I'm sorry; I don't like all this."

"I forgive you, Joey, for your part in this. I know you're different than they are. You can see the wrong in all of this. I wish they could."

"Where's my saddle? Are you goin' to bring it to me, or not?" Charlie yelled.

"Yeah, I'm gonna bring it to ya!"

"Thank you, Joey, for saying what you said. It means a lot to me."

"It's how I feel. I don't like it here anymore." He picked up Charlie's blanket and saddle and headed toward the cabin.

She watched him walk away and wondered what would happen to him after all of this was over.

"Here's your saddle, Charlie."

"Put it behind me, so I can sit up."

He set it on the stretcher just behind Charlie. "Is that good?"

"Yes, thank you, Joey." Being somewhat helpless gave Charlie time to think about his loss of independence and that if he was a friend he might have a friend. He thought he'd save the rest of the laudanum and turn his attention to the whiskey if there was some to be had.

The pain had been steadily increasing. He could feel pressure building up in his hip. He undid his pants and pushed them down enough to examine himself. He discovered that the hip was swollen with a large black and blue area covering it. Charlie realized that he was bleeding inside that part of his hip. It must have broken when he heard it pop. His attempt at sitting up lasted only a few minutes. He pushed his saddle aside with great difficulty and lay back, turning his face to the small fire.

His mounting fears had a powerful grip on his mind. What would he do if he could no longer walk, ride, or drive a wagon? He wasn't able to go off into the woods and relieve himself, no one was going to take care of him or give him a handout; he didn't have any friends. He was quickly becoming useless in his own eyes, and he felt that he had no place to turn.

Charlie raised his voice and asked Lester, "Do you have a bottle of whiskey to soothe my pain?"

To his surprise, Lester walked over and handed him a bottle.

"Thanks, this will help," Charlie commented.

"I don't need it. Anyways, I need a clear head for tomorrow." He then returned to the door of the cabin to stand guard.

"Do you want something to eat? I can serve you some of this vegetable soup and a john cake?" Emma asked Charlie. She had been watching in silence as she sipped her own hot cup of soup and enjoyed the warmth of the fire that was taking the edge off the cool night air.

"No, woman, I don't. The pain has stolen my appetite." Instead, he tried to prop his head up and take a drink of whiskey.

Emma felt emotionally drained, and all she wanted was to sleep peacefully through the night. Her mind was overstimulated with the single thought of what tomorrow would bring. She knew with confidence that the answer to all of this was about to be given and that thought disturbed her greatly. After all this time, she still couldn't put the pieces of the puzzle together. What was all of this about?

She made her way to the cot in the cabin, which sat in the left corner away from the window, protecting her from the morning sun. She lay down and straightened her soiled dress to make herself a bit more comfortable, pulling the blanket over her. The ceiling didn't provide the peaceful view that the starry night sky did. She wanted to sleep outside by the fire except Lester wouldn't allow it.

She closed her eyes and prayed. *Heavenly Father, you know me and my situation. I need Your strength and courage. I don't know what is coming, and I fear it. Forgive me for having this fear. You said that prefect love casts out all fear. Please fill me with Your love, peace, and strength so that I can endure what You are allowing me to go through, for whatever the reason is, my Lord. Please place Your angels around me and bless Loretta with the Holy Spirit and with Your mighty hand of protection. I miss her so much, Lord. I want to hold her once more. And Will, the only man I've ever really loved—please bring him here to take me home. Please Father, my heart is breaking. I need You because without You I can do nothing, and I confess that I'm unworthy to ask anything of You. Father, it's Jesus who is worthy, pure, and clean, and I ask all of this in*

His name, which is above every name, amen. She wiped her eyes dry with her dress sleeves and shortly fell off to sleep.

As the night wore on, the men also went to sleep. Suddenly they awoke to the sound of a single gunshot that rumbled through the cabin from the outdoors. Lester jumped to his feet and grabbed his pistol, which was never far from his side. As he ran through the dark in the direction of the shot, he barely missed the doorframe with his left shoulder. He reached the fire that was now reduced to coals and spoke to Charlie, but he received no reply. He quickly scrambled to find a few pieces of kindling to start a fire and provide much-needed light.

Emma brought the unlit candle from off the small makeshift table in the cabin. A piece of kindling was lightly burning now, which allowed Lester to light the candle. As the light penetrated the darkness, they could see the reason for the gunshot.

Emma stood quietly as Lester knelt down on one knee beside Charlie. Charlie had placed his hat over his face and held it tight with his left hand. He had then taken his pistol in his right hand and shot himself in the heart. It appeared as if he had died immediately. By this time Joey stood in the glow of the fire, wondering why Charlie would do such a thing.

Joey spoke his thoughts, "What made him do it, Lester?"

"I'm guessing it's because he didn't want to be an invalid. He didn't think he could earn a living that way, and he had no one to care for him, no family, nothing. So he took care of the situation the way he saw best."

"It makes no sense to me," Joey said.

"It doesn't to me, either. It's not the way I'd take care of it, even an invalid can make a living."

Joey picked up the empty whiskey bottle and said, "Look, he drank it all."

"Yeah, it gave him the courage to pull the trigger, plus he was taking that laudanum." Lester picked up Charlie's blanket and covered him with it. "After sunrise we'll bury him. It's too bad he did this because he could have made it if he'd tried. He got under my skin at times, and we did have the falling out, but we were friends. There's nothing more we can do here, so let's get some more sleep."

Emma was wide awake as the sun peeked in through the cabin window. Lester yawned and sat up. Putting his feet on the floor, he pulled his boots on, grabbed his gun and shirt, and headed outside. He roused Joey to help with digging the grave.

Emma wanted to start breakfast. There were provisions, but she lacked eggs, milk, and a few other desired items to make the food she wanted. She was tired and didn't really care, so reheating the soup and the john cakes would suffice. She built a fire and sat down to relax, hoping that today was the day that Will would come and take her home. The men had finished burying Charlie and were headed Emma's way.

"I smell soup," Joey said.

They both sat down and waited to be served. As she served the soup, she asked, "Did you mark his grave with a cross or something?"

"I know he's there. He doesn't need a cross. And don't be praying over him, either. He didn't believe in all that Christian stuff!" Lester snapped.

"I thought it would be nice if his grave was marked, something to remember him by, that's all," she said in a soft and subdued voice.

Lester mumbled something and with the little finger of his right hand rubbed his left eye. Grabbing a john cake out of the pan, he picked up his hot soup and headed for the cabin to eat alone.

"He gets mad a lot about nothing," Joey said.

Emma nodded her head in agreement as she continued to remind herself that this day was already packed with enough of life's heartaches, as she thought about Charlie. Lester's little tantrum wasn't worth considering.

Joey had since finished eating and tending to the horses. He now sat in the sun against the cabin with his eyes closed, relaxing. Emma sat and, with great effort, sorted through her thoughts—they were like a wagon wheel turning around and around without an end.

Just then Lester came running around the corner and said, "Woman, someone is coming up the trail. Get in the cabin, and stay out of sight until I tell you to do otherwise." He ran a short distance into the woods, traveling parallel to the trail. He stopped and waited for the coming riders about a quarter of a mile down the trail.

As the riders came into view, Lester recognized Peter Wyler, so he stepped onto the trail. "You're late, Wyler," Lester said with a straight face.

"Just by a day, Lester, that's all. My brother Allen has been sick, so we stopped and rested for a few days in Yreka."

"Good to meet ya, Allen Wyler," Lester said, addressing the other man.

"Likewise, but the last name is Hoffman. Wyler was just a cover," he said through a cough.

Lester didn't care what his name was. "Let's talk about payment. The woman is here and untouched as you requested."

"If you have the sheriff, then the job's done, but not until I have him standing in front of me, or is that something you forgot, Lester?"

"I don't remember that being part of the deal."

"The woman and her man go together; that's the agreement. I don't pay for a job half done any more than you do. Did you make it easy for him to track you?"

"I didn't nail signs to the trees if that's what you're asking, but I'm sure I left tracks behind us," Lester said.

"Well then, you shouldn't have anything to worry about. I'm sure he is hot on your trail. Once he arrives and we have them both, you will get paid. We have an understanding now, don't we, Lester," Allen said as he pushed his hat back and wiped the sweat from his forehead.

Lester understood, but he wanted his money now, so he thought he would try another way.

"Yeah, I remember now. Follow me up the hill."

"Where is she?" Allen asked as they approached the cabin.

"Inside. I'll get her," Lester responded.

He stuck his head inside and looked over at Emma who was standing in the shadowed corner. "Get outside; there's someone who wants to see you."

Emma walked through the doorway into the sunlight, praying under her breath, "Please, Jesus, help me."

"Brother, it looks like you've got what you wished for. It's her."

"It is! Do you remember me, Emma?"

Emma stood still—she was in shock, not really believing what she was seeing. Large tears appeared in her eyes and rolled down her cheeks. A small gasp escaped from her lips. "Allen, is it you?" She put her hand to her mouth and tried to back away. Lester grabbed her by the arms and held her still.

Allen climbed down from his horse and walked toward her, stopping a foot in front of her. He stood in silence for a moment, looking her over. He took a deep breath and said, "You're a little older, but you haven't changed much, Emma. You're still pretty … you're still pretty." He ran the back of his right hand slowly down the side of her right cheek.

He had changed with the passing of time. He now walked with a slight limp, and she could smell liquor on his breath. The change was also one of the heart, not of the body alone. He was hard and cold, she could tell—even the air around him felt tense.

"What are you doing here, Allen, and why?" She tried to hide her tears from him by covering her face. Her efforts met with little success, seeing that Lester was still holding her arms tightly.

"Let her loose!" Peter interjected. He climbed down off his mount and gave Lester a threatening look.

"Why am I doing this?" Allen said with anger. "Why am I doing this?" He backed away from her and raised his arms into the air, then slowly turned around. "Does that answer your question?"

"No! I don't understand," Emma cried loudly.

"It's my broken body. My years in that stinking prison thinking about you, wondering." A number of hard coughs that came from deep within his lungs interrupted his long awaited and carefully thought through speech. He continued as if the interruption was a normal occurrence. "I wondered if you were happy, healthy, and free, because I wasn't!

"When I finally located you, I got more than I expected—a nice little house on the edge of town, a cute little girl, and a lawman for a husband. Think of that, you with a lawman. If people knew where you've been and what you've done, you wouldn't be looked upon as being so prim and proper, would you!"

"I've changed, I'm not the same as I was. I believe in Jesus now, and He's forgiven me for everything I've done wrong. Please stop this, Allen, and let me go home!"

"Yes, I found that out, too. You've become a Christian, and all of your sins are forgiven. Everything is fine now because you're all lily white. What about the difficult times you put me through, the pain you caused me? How does your Jesus justify that, and how do I gain back all those lost years that could've been sweet like yours?"

"I'm sorry, Allen, for hurting you. Please forgive me for all I've done. I was just a young girl, and I did what you told me to do. I ran for my life," she said.

"Yes, you ran for your life, and I lost mine. That night when we were robbing that jewelry store on the second floor, you knocked over an oil lamp that in turn knocked the small display case off the counter which hit the floor with a crash. Do you remember what happened next?"

"I just remember running out of the store and down the stairs. Then I climbed on my horse and rode until I couldn't ride anymore. You told me to run, so I did. Why didn't you run with me?"

"Because that job was the biggest one I had ever had, and I wasn't going to leave it all behind. I thought I had enough time to grab a few more jewels, but someone came running up the stairs and I was forced to escape by jumping out the side window. When I hit the ground, I broke my leg and that's how they caught me, then I ended up in prison. If you hadn't been so stupid, so careless, and made all that noise none of this would had happened. It's all your fault that my life is the way it is!"

Emma just lowered her head and cried. She knew it wasn't all true. She had knocked over the lamp and gave them away, but his broken leg and prison time were his doing. It was his great love for money that stole his freedom and all those years. His mind was twisted; his imagination had become his reality. He truly believed that his ruined life was her fault.

"And I can imagine that you have this lawman wrapped around your finger just like you had me back then. I suppose he's going to come riding in here and swoop you up in his arms and ride away with you, but I have news for you. That's not going to happen!" Allen grabbed hold of her right arm and, looking her in the eyes, said, "Come with me to the top of the hill."

"Stop it, Allen! You're hurting me." She stiffened up her body in an attempt to resist his tight grasp.

He jerked her forward and said demandingly, "Come with me!"

Joey jumped up from where he had been sitting against the cabin wall and rushed toward Allen. "Don't you hurt her!" he yelled.

Peter Hoffman drew his pistol and quickly fired a shot in Joey's direction. Emma flinched in fear and screamed, "Nooooo ... !"

Chapter Seven

Like Brothers

Pulling into Yreka was a sight for Will's tired eyes. The city looked like it was going to live up to its reputation of being full of life of every kind.

"Is anyone hungry?" Yann asked.

Tanger echoed his own desire to eat by saying, "Yeah, follow me, men." He led them through a maze of streets, stopping in front of a reasonably new one-story house. Tanger jumped down from his horse, tied him to the post, and turned and said, "This is where I stay with my ma and her friends when I'm in town. You said you were hungry, didn't you? Then come on, let's eat."

The two quickly followed Tanger through the front door, which opened to a sparsely furnished foyer. Will looked down at the oval rug he was standing on which was a mixture of browns and greens with a touch of red thrown in as a highlight. Tanger disappeared for a moment and then returned with his mother and a young woman named Leah. Her husband, Robert, wasn't home at the time—he was a mechanic around the city. After everyone was properly introduced, Tanger asked, "Leah, would you mind feeding three very hungry men? We'll replace all the supplies we eat up."

Leah and his mother, Cora, removed themselves from the dining room where the men had taken their seats to the kitchen to start the meal. The topic of conversation for the women was about Yann being Chinese and how Robert would deal with having him stay in his home. The thought of it made both of them stressed and a little concerned how he might react when he walked in the front door, which would be soon.

"I think we should stay and really search this town for clues, probably for two days. I'm impressed something is going to turn up. We can split up as we usually do. I can take the main streets and sheriff's office. Yann, the Chinese section. Tanger, you know the city and what would be the best areas to check out, so you take the back streets," said Will.

Yann interrupted Will's planning session. "When I met your mother and Leah, I could sense the tension," he said to Tanger. "I don't want to be the cause of any trouble, so when I finish eating, which I appreciate, I will go to my own people and see what I can learn."

"They tend not to be that way. I think it's Robert who's giving them the neckache without him even being here. It would be better if you didn't stay or sleep under the same roof with him. I'm sorry; it's not what I wanted," Tanger replied.

Leah entered the room with a plate of bread and set it down on the table along with a bowl of stew for each of them. "I did the best I could with the time I was given. I overheard your conversation, and Yann, if it was my choice, you could stay, but I have no say-so in matters like this. It's up to my husband. I'm sorry, Yann; you're so congenial."

"Thank you for your kindness, Leah," Yann said.

She nodded and sat down next to Tanger. "Eat up," she said.

Cora soon emerged from the kitchen with an orange for each of them. They were large and fresh looking. "Enjoy them," she said. She maneuvered her way past the chair to where Tanger was sitting. She stopped and put her arm around his neck, kissing him on the forehead. "Eric, where are you off to this time?"

"Ma, when I introduced you to Will, I didn't tell you that he's the sheriff of Stone Ridge. His wife was kidnapped, and we're going after her. We are hoping to find her and the men soon. He wants to stay here for a few days and see what we can find out in town, and then we're on our way north."

"That could be dangerous, son."

"True, Ma, but she's his wife. If I was in his shoes, I'd want them to help me out. It's what I need to do. We've become like brothers the three of us," he said.

"You know I love you, son, and I want you to do what's right. This looks like the right thing to do, so I'll pray for God's safety as you continue your search. Please tell me, where did the three of you meet?"

"At the trading post. I talked to Marie Rose, and she's doin' fine," Tanger replied. "She said to say hi."

Will had finished his meal and was antsy to get going. "Are we ready to start the search?" he interjected.

"No, but I guess I can eat more later," Tanger replied. "I'll need to show you the way, Yann. You could run into trouble by yourself."

Tanger turned to address his mother before leaving the table. "Ma, we can talk about all this later. In fact, I want to tell you about a girl I met at Fort Reading. Her name is Kate, and she has a young son named Clay. I think you would really like her."

She nodded in agreement. He picked up his orange, shoved another spoonful of stew into his mouth, stood up, grabbed a large piece of bread, and put on his hat. He then headed for the door. His two partners followed him out the front door.

Once outside Max eyed them and jumped up to follow his master. Tanger rubbed Max's forehead as he asked Will, "Can you find Main Street?"

"Yeah, I can."

"When you reach Main Street, turn right; the sheriff's office is down and to the left."

"Will, we can take the horses to the stable on the way," Tanger said as an afterthought.

"Fine," Will responded as he rested his rifle on his right shoulder and headed toward Main Street. He prayed as he approached the first person in a long line of people to ask. He received the basic answer. "No, I haven't seen anyone like that." *What's a few hundred no's when the reward for one yes is so great.* He could ask the same question all day long because the Lord had given him a good strong voice.

"The stable is just up ahead, Yann," Tanger said. A sign that read *Harry's* hung over the barn's double doors. They dismounted and led their horses inside. "Hi, Harry, how ya doin' these days?"

"All right. Business is strong. What can I do for you, and what is this Chinaman doing here? You know I don't take any of their horses in."

"Harry, one question at a time. I'm bedding down these four, and this one is for sale with the saddle. She's a fine mare, and take a look at the tooling on that saddle."

"I'll look at her. Now what about him? You know I don't like to ask the same question too many times," Harry said, folding his arms across his chest.

"He works for me, and the horse he's ridin' is also mine."

"Since when did you start hiring people and providing them with a horse too?"

"I'm tracking kidnappers north of here, and he's a good tracker, Harry. That's why he's with me."

"Why four horses, then?"

"Question after question, Harry! The roan belongs to the sheriff along with the bay. It's the sheriff I'm workin' for!"

"What sheriff is that, Tanger?"

"Will Jacobs from Stone Ridge. Now do you want to care for the animals and buy the mare or not?"

"Yes to both. I'll give you two hundred for her."

"She and the saddle will bring four hundred, and you know it, Harry," Tanger countered. "The lowest I'll go is three hundred. There are a few other stables around here, you know."

"All right, Tanger, three hundred it is," Harry said with a frown.

"I need one more thing. I'd like to sleep here for the night."

"And I suppose that's free of charge, Tanger?"

"Think of me as your security guard."

"The things I do for you. Sometimes I worry about myself."

"Harry, have you seen three men—one tall, two short—with a woman in her late twenties. She's five seven, pretty, brown hair?"

"No, I haven't seen them," Harry replied.

"What time are you closing?"

"Don't worry about that, just come next door and I'll let you in."

"Harry, I'll take the money in cash."

"I figured that much, can I give it to you tomorrow?"

"Yes, you can. See you later on."

Tanger walked out as Yann hurried to keep up with him. Due to Tanger's long strides, sometimes he fell behind a hair. "Yann, do you think you'll stay with your people tonight or at the stable?"

"That depends if I can find a place to sleep or not," Yann said.

"As I said earlier, if you get caught out after dark, you could end up takin' a good beating, and I don't want that."

"I'll do my best."

"Turn left at the end of this street, and it will lead you to Miner Street. Chinatown starts there. Bring me back some good news, would you."

He smiled and said, "I'll try." As he entered Chinatown, a home away from home, he was refreshed by the sights and sounds of home and the aroma of familiar food. To greet a man in his own language was one more reminder of what he was lacking. In some ways he didn't fit in—his hair and dress were no longer in harmony with his people. He had changed. He enjoyed the western styles, one of which was having hair on his head.

He spoke to dozens of people on the various streets and in the small shops that were mingled in along the way. He received polite and not so polite answers "No, I haven't," and "Why do you ask, anyway?" He was starting to doubt if they would ever find Will's wife. Were they having any more success than he?

He entered a shop squeezed between two other buildings as if it was an afterthought. It was narrow, long, and very crowded with goods covering the floor and hanging from the ceiling. Varieties of dried fish, dried squid, and other creatures of the sea also joined the items that hung from the ceiling. The customers were dressed in their native black pajamas. Every man wore a hat—some were short while others were tall. If anyone had removed their hat, it would have revealed a nearly smooth shaven head with a long braided piece of hair that grew from the back of the head.

Yann moved through the narrow aisles asking questions that were often ignored.

As he approached the counter, the man standing behind it said, "You're new here, aren't you? What is it that you're looking for? Goods, pleasure, family, friends—whatever it is I can help you with it." At the end of his sales pitch, he quickly added, "Did you just get off the ship?"

"No, I've been here for awhile. I'm looking for three American men, two are short and one is tall; they're riding with a woman who is five feet seven inches tall. The men kidnapped her. Have you or anyone else you know seen or heard anything?"

"Why are you, being Chinese, looking for them?"

"I'm riding with the men who are trying to find the woman, that's why I'm asking the question!" Yann said.

"No, I can't help you, and they would not help you if this woman was Chinese, that I am sure of."

"Not all Americans hate us, some of them understand. Thank you for your time," said Yann, then turning, he headed for the door. The street was busy, and the day was getting on. He thought he'd check the next street over before heading back to the stable.

From across the street two men approached. They stopped and leaned against the building, as if to rest, a short distance ahead of Yann. As he neared, they stepped in front of him. Yann had seen this type before—young men in their early twenties filled with rice wine and not fond of hard work with too much free time on their hands. So they took to harassing strangers.

"What do you want?" Yann asked.

"We were admiring your American cloths and hair. You are Chinese, aren't you?"

"Yes, of course I am. American clothes are practical for many things," Yann replied.

The two men looked at each other and laughed. The one standing to his left said, "Yeah, if you want to be like them. Do you also believe in Christianity?"

Yann found himself wanting to say "Yes, I do," which was a huge revelation even to himself. Instead, "No, I don't. I'm not a Christian" flowed from his lips.

"Tell me the truth! What is it that you really believe!" the same man said as he stepped a little closer.

Yann didn't comment. Instead, he moved to the right to go around them. But he felt a hand take hold of his left arm at that moment. "Where are you going? I have more to say to you!"

In one quick smooth motion, he reached over with his right hand and took hold of the man's left hand, bending his wrist back as he turned to face him. Yann said determinedly, "Don't do that! I have done nothing to you. Now go and pour your rice wine on the ground!" He let go of the man's hand and repeated "Go!" The two young men quickly turned and lost themselves in the mingling crowd.

Now that they were gone, he was left with his thoughts. He wasn't troubled by the two reckless men; it was the words, "Yes, I do," that bothered him. He wasn't being honest with himself. Since he and Will rode out of Marysville, life had taken on a new twist. On top of everything that had transpired, he was now beginning to accept Christ for who He was—the Son of the living God.

He stopped and looked up at the sign that hung above his head. It read *Lee's*. He could smell the food as a man opened the door and walked out. He would love to have some rice, boiled fish with vegetables, and a cup of tea or two, but he felt he should catch up with the others at the stable before darkness took them captive for the night.

As he continued walking, he could see more clearly that unintentional changes had taken place in his life. He lived less like his forefathers than ever before. He really was becoming a man in the middle.

Yann didn't see his partners as he reached the stable. The owner was sitting on a chair in front of the open doors. "Your boss isn't back yet, Chinaman. If you're goin' to stay here for the night, you can clean the stalls for the privilege of it. You'll find the shovel and pitchfork over there in the corner, and you'd better hurry before you lose what light is left." He then put his head down and went back to his whittling.

This wasn't his first choice for an evening of entertainment. He could use the time more effectively by planning Sanne's escape from China. But it didn't seem as if he had a choice. He started with the stalls that housed their own horses first and worked from there.

Later, as he was relaxing comfortably in the hayloft, he heard Harry let Will and Tanger in.

"Yann, are you here! It's us," Tanger said loudly as he held the oil lantern above his head.

"Yes, up here in the loft."

"Come on down; I've got some hot stew for you. I thought you might be hungry."

As Yann came down the ladder, Tanger informed him that the food had come from his mother.

"So, did you have any success? Did you get any information?"

"None at all. I did learn though that a man like me is standing in the middle."

"Explain yourself," Will said.

"Look at me—I'm Chinese, but I'm dressed like you, and my hair is growing out. My people don't like what they see; they feel that I have turned against them. They don't understand. I felt it a good part of the day as I spoke with them. I was also stopped by two men who were looking for a fight. They harassed me over my hair and clothes."

"It's hard to be in the middle, Yann. I wish I had the answer," Will replied. "Come on, sit down and eat."

They ate in silence for a few minutes, and then Will began talking about the plans for the next day. "I figure we can ride out about noon tomorrow. That will give us enough time to finish up here. The sheriff told me that if we need to stop over for the night with the prisoners, he will give us a hand. And he gave me an extra pair of handcuffs, so now I have three pairs

"I think we should just shoot them all and bring their bodies back for identification. Let's make it easy, Will," Tanger said.

"Before I was a Christian, I would have done the same, but not now. This has to be done safe and smooth. I don't want Emma hurt. This must be heartbreaking for her, and she doesn't need to see those men dying around her."

"Let me ask you this. What are you going to do if they draw on you and give you no other choice? Are you gonna stand there like a duck? What good are you to Emma dead, answer me that?" Tanger said with a tone of irritation in his voice.

"If I have no other choice, I'll shoot them, but I don't want to. Tanger, I can't take a chance on Emma being hurt. You know how I feel. We've been over this before!"

"Suit yourself, Will. Have it your way. But I'll tell you right now, if any of them points a gun at me with the intention of pulling the trigger, I'm shooting first, and that's the way it is. Do you understand?"

"Yeah, I understand what you're saying, but I need you to corporate with me for Emma's sake and safety," Will said sharply.

The three became quiet for a time until Tanger stood up and said, "I'm goin' to check on Pik. He needs a brushing."

Like an echo from the past, Yann commented, "This is reminiscent."

"He's a good man. He'll cool down in a bit," Will said.

"Will, I need to tell you what happened today. When the two guys harassed me on the street, one of them asked me if I believed in Christianity. My answer was 'No, I don't,' but that wasn't the truth in my heart. Will, in my heart I said 'Yes, I do.' I keep asking myself when did this happen, when did it start? I only know that I'm starting to believe in Christ. Something has changed inside of me."

Will looked up to the ceiling of the barn and said, "The Lord has great power and wisdom. He has done this in you. He has given you the gift of faith. Samuel had a strong influence on you. I could tell that something had changed when you got back and told us about everything that had happened. Now it is time for you to trust in the Lord, pray to Him, and learn from His Word. Your new life has just started. Be thankful and enjoy the things that the Lord is going to do in you. Can I pray for you, Yann?" he asked.

"Yes."

Will raised his head toward the ceiling again, and in his mind's eye he could see the stars above. "Mighty Father, thank you for loving us, for giving us Jesus, and for the forgiveness of all of our sins. Thank you for changing Yann's heart. Father, I ask You to please bless him with Your spirit and bless Sanne. Keep her safe. I ask this, Father, in Jesus' name, amen."

Will opened his eyes and told Yann, "The Lord has shown you great favor. I don't know what He has planned for your life, but I know He has a plan. He wouldn't have freed you from Seen or sent Samuel to help if your life didn't have a purpose."

"Yann! Can you shoot this bow?" Tanger hollered from the back of the stable, interrupting their conversation.

Yann turned his head in Tanger's direction and said, "Yes, I can. What makes you ask?"

"Well, it belonged to Seen, so I thought you might be keeping it for a souvenir, that's all."

"Bring me the bow and arrows, Tanger, and I'll show you the answer to your question."

Yann stood up and looked for a good spot to demonstrate his archery skills.

He eyed one of the posts that gave support to the hayloft overhead. The post had a nail half driven into it that was used to hang things from. He found a rag as he walked toward the post, and he hung it on the nail. Walking back to where he had been, he met Tanger who handed him the bow.

"Do you see the small rag twice the size of a playing card hanging from the nail? That's the new home of these three arrows," Yann said.

"If we're going to depend on each other, we should know what we're depending on, right? So show us," Tanger said.

Yann let all three arrows fly in quick succession with all three hitting their mark.

"Not bad, but it could be beginner's luck," Tanger said with a small grin.

"Do you still need convincing? Then try this one … and this one …" The next two arrows both found a place on the white rag. "Need I shoot anymore?"

"I knew you could do it. I just wanted to see you do it again, that's all," Tanger said.

"I've shot since I was a child. Sons are expected to master the art of self-defense, and I studied very hard during my youth."

Tanger pulled his knife from its sheath and handed it to Yann as he said, "How's your knife throwin' ability?"

"About the same," he said as he threw the knife approximately six feet and firmly stuck it in the nearest post.

Tanger nodded his head in silent approval. He was very impressed. He pulled his knife from the post and took a comfortable place next to Will. They talked awhile about their women, their dreams, and the dangers they might run into shortly.

"So what makes you think we're goin' to find something tomorrow?" Tanger asked.

"I don't know, but I do think we'll find something. Maybe something like the seashell or something better, I just don't know. But I feel that we're really close, closer than we've ever been. That's the best I can tell you, brother. Now enough talk, I'm getting some sleep." Will stood up and headed for the ladder.

After Will left, Yann turned to Tanger and said, "Can you tell me a little more about Kate, if you don't mind?"

"There's not much more to tell. She's about six foot tall and from German descent. She's a handsome woman with big blue eyes. I find when I'm around her I have peace and I can talk to her, not like most women, where I have nothin' to say. I didn't tell you about Clay, her son. He's eight, I think. He's smart, polite, and does what he's asked without talking back to you. I've got a spot in my heart for him already, and it has been growin'. I miss them both. Like I said, they're waiting for me back at Fort Reading. I hope Will is right about being close to finding Emma because I'm ready to head back to the fort and court Kate."

"I wish I had the promise of seeing my dear Sanne when this is all over," Yann responded.

"If I could, I would help you find her, but China is a long ways from here," Tanger said with emotion.

"I believe you, and I may need your help in finding a safe and peaceful place to live when all this is over. I feel like I've been placed in a box and as long as I obey I will do just fine, but that's not living." After stating that, his mind was impressed with the thought *Pray for the wisdom and faith to follow Me wherever I lead.* It startled him, and he sat looking at the hay-covered ground as he thought over the words.

"It's time for me to turn in," Tanger said.

"I should, too," Yann replied.

❧❧❧❧❧❧

Morning came quickly, and Yann was the first one up. He watered and fed the horses and gave them a quick brushing. They seemed to hold their heads a little higher with pride after the brushing. He then sat down to wait for his sleeping friends. A few moments later, Harry unlocked the stable doors and swung them open.

He eyed Yann and said, "Where's your boss!"

Tanger gave Yann no time to answer. He hollered on his way down the ladder, "What do you need, Harry?"

"What time you headed out? I have the money for ya. I can take the boarding fee out of what I owe ya, if ya like."

"What are you chargin' me for all this fine service, Harry?"

"Tanger, don't try that on me. Ya know I get ten dollars a day for each horse. That's thirty dollars for the three of ya."

"Right, that's if you water and feed them. Yann did all of that yesterday and this morning before you got here, plus we guarded your place. You know I'm right, Harry. I'll give ya twenty dollars for everything. You give me the rest in cash and that will settle it. You know you're getting' a good deal, Harry." By this time Will had his boots on and was down the ladder waiting for Tanger, hoping soon to be on his way.

"Who owns this place, me or you, anyway?" Harry asked.

"Maybe I will someday, Harry, and maybe I'll give it to my son," Tanger said.

"Are you sane? Why, you don't even have a wife, let alone a son."

"Now pay up, Harry," Tanger said with his hand out.

"We're heading out about noon, so we'll see you then," Will said.

"That's not soon enough for me. You guys give me a headache," Harry replied.

As they walked out of the stable, Yann said, "I don't know what to do with myself."

"You can come with me. I have some side streets left to check, then we can catch up with Will."

Will nodded his head and said, "I'll see you later."

It wasn't more than fifteen minutes of straight "No, I can't help ya with that" when Tanger saw a tall older man who looked familiar. He ran down the street, grabbed the man's left arm, and spun him around. The moment had come that he really didn't believe ever would. Years of anger came pouring out like a flood upon the unsuspecting man.

"I never thought I'd see you again, you useless uncle of mine. You ran off on us. Your brother was barely dead when you left me and Ma alone. She got the fever later and almost died. She's never been the same since. You coward— you ran out on us!" Tanger was now shaking him and yelling, "You old fool! What do you have to say for yourself?"

"Eric," the man said in surprise, "Let go of me. You have no right to treat me like this! He was my brother; I loved him and looked up to him. After he was dead, I didn't know what else to do. I was confused. Do you think you're the only one who had it hard all these years? I miss him, too. He was my hero even though he was my baby brother. I'm sorry I ran out on you and your ma; I really am. Is your ma still alive? If she is, I'd like to see her and apologize."

Tanger finally let go of his uncle's shirt. He then sat down on a bench in front of the building where they stood. "She's alive. She lives a few streets over. You and me were close. We did a lot of things together, then you ran off."

His uncle straightened his shirt and hat as he stepped over to the bench. "Eric, I'm sorry for all the hurt I've caused you. Can you forgive me?"

Tanger raised his head and said, "Do you mean it from your heart, because you're asking a big thing? All those years full of pain and anger; it's not an easy thing to put aside."

"Yes, I mean it. I thought about it a hundred times over the years. It's time for healing, Eric. This didn't happen by accident today. Take me to your ma so I can tell her how I feel?"

"OK, I'll take you there. Follow me." As Tanger led the way, they walked in silence. Yann had witnessed a miracle in forgiveness. He now hoped that Tanger would receive God's forgiveness as Will and Samuel had hoped for him.

When they reached the house, Tanger said, "I'm not goin' in with you. You and Ma should talk alone." He opened the door and said, "Ma, there's an old friend who wants to talk to you. It's important, but I feel you should face this skeleton without me here. I'll talk to you later."

"Thanks, Eric," his uncle said as he offered his hand as a token of sincerity. Tanger accepted it and then turned to walk away.

As they strolled down the street, Yann spoke up, "You've done the right thing. Your heart will be lighter."

"It wasn't easy, but when he asked me to forgive him, I had no good reason not to. I think that maybe my hate was more anger and hurt than anything else. I hope I did the right thing."

They turned a corner and headed toward Main Street. Yann stopped two Chinese men with arms full of dirty laundry and questioned them as Tanger walked on. Yann ran to catch up with Tanger who had just finished talking to a young man at a hitching post who also had nothing to report.

"Have you seen Max since we left the stable?" Tanger asked as Yann joined him.

"No, I kind of forgot about him with everything goin' on."

"I should keep a better watch over him, but he is such a good dog that I just assume he is always close by."

As they turned the corner onto Main Street, they saw a number of curious onlookers who had formed a small crowd. They heard a man say, "You may have to shoot the dog to stop him."

But Tanger knew that growl. "Let me through," he said. Sure enough, it was Max. His hair was standing up on the back of his neck, and he was showing off his beautiful white teeth. He was certainly annoyed over something. "Max, it's all right. Stop it!" Tanger said quickly before the situation escalated.

"Is that your dog?" a man asked as he pointed to Max with a club in his right hand. The club looked like it was about two feet long.

"Yeah, he is. What did you do to get him stirred up like this?" Tanger asked.

"I don't like dogs, especially big ones," he said.

"Mister, I don't like the way you've bothered my dog. You did well not to take that bad advice given you, because shootin' my dog is like stealin' my horse. I know my dog. If you don't bother him, he won't bother you, kind of the way I am."

"You keep that dog away from me, you hear me!" the man said in an elevated tone.

"If you'd put that club away, you'd do a lot better," responded Tanger. He backed away from the man and stepped into the street with Max close by his side. "Max, I got you out of this one. From now on you have to stay by my side."

Tanger turned and spoke to Yann. "I guess we need to keep asking around. I sure hope we find Emma soon. I'm gettin' tired of asking the same questions over and over. I've already asked some people twice, and they've looked at me like I was losing my mind. Maybe there's some truth to it. I talk to Pik and Max like they're people, and sometimes I think they answer me. Am I crazy for courting Kate? That thought crossed my mind yesterday."

"You're not losing your mind, and courting is a good thing. A man must learn and grow. Do you want to be the same ten years from now?" Yann asked.

"Well, since you put it that way, no."

"Now talking to animals, that's not a problem, but if they start talking back, let me know what they say, it could be interesting," Yann said with a laugh.

৵৵৵৵৵৵

"Tanger! Over here to your left," Monty beckoned.

Tanger waved at him as he stopped to talk to a man and woman crossing the street. The question rolled from his tongue automatically.

"I'm sorry. We arrived only a few hours ago. I wish I could give you the information you're looking for," the stranger answered.

"Thanks," said Tanger as he turned to see what his old friend Monty had to say.

Monty was a short and slightly rounded man who was bright, well-educated and highly intuitive. He now stood before Tanger in a pale yellow and brown suit, which was too much for the California climate. It gave him the feeling of dressing snappy, when in actuality he looked like a dude. He quickly spoke up in his usual manner as he wiped the sweat from his brow and the tip of his nose. He then repositioned his hat.

"I've been looking for you for weeks. I have three wagons that need repair. How soon can you start the job? These drivers of mine are so careless I've considered dismissing them and hiring new ones. Do you know what it would cost a man like me to hire older and truly skilled drivers? More than I'd care to pay, I can tell you that much," Monty complained.

"If that's the case, you'll have to keep hirin' me to fix them, won't you? I have another job right now, Monty. I can't help you. What I do need is information, now think hard."

"What kind, Tanger?"

"I'm looking for three men, one is taller than the other two and one is named Charlie, he's one of the short men, and he drags a spur. The woman who is with them has brown hair and is good lookin'. But she's been kidnapped by the men. I'm riding with Jacobs, the sheriff of Stone Ridge. The woman is his wife; her name is Emma. Can you help me with this, Monty?"

"Tanger, I haven't heard a word from anyone on this one. I don't think they came into town. You know the way I am; I know when someone dies and when someone is born and everything in-between. My sense is that they bypassed us here. I will keep me ears open. I'm sorry to disappoint you, my friend. I can see this is very important to you."

"You can only tell me what you know, Monty. Thanks."

"Hey you, the tall one!" Tanger turned his head to the right to hear it repeated. "That's right, you the tall one."

"What can I do for you, old timer?" Tanger asked.

"I overheard you talkin', and I think I can help you. My name is Ned."

"Ned, I'm Tanger," he said with a nod.

"Yesterday I was headin' in from the north on the main road. It was mid-afternoon, and I met two men. One was ridin', and one was in one of those Indian travois. He stopped me and said his hip was killin' him with pain and did I have any laudanum. I said 'Yes, I do.' He paid me a twenty dollar gold piece for it."

"What's the point, Ned?" Tanger asked impatiently.

"I'm getting to it! His name was Charlie, and when he reached in his pocket to get the gold piece, this note fell on the ground."

"What note!"

"I'll give it to ya." He reached into his coat pocket and handed the note to Tanger. "I don't hardly read, but it says somethin' about a woman and meetin' them north."

Tanger quickly read it and said, "You did better than you think. That's what it says. Yann, we've got them! I know pretty much where they are. We've got to find Will!"

"Wait! Don't you think the note is worth somethin'?" Ned asked.

Yann quickly handed Ned a ten dollar gold piece and followed after Tanger.

They looked up and down Main Street, but they didn't see any sign of Will. "He may have headed back toward your mother's house," Yann stated. "Let's look in that direction." They rapidly scanned the passersby as they ran down the streets to Cora's house, only to find that he had already come and gone. Tanger led the run toward the stable, the only place he could think of that Will might be. As they approached the two wide double doors of the stable, they found Harry sitting in his old wooden chair soaking up the noonday sun.

"What's the emergency? Harry asked.

"Is Will inside?"

"Yeah, he's saddling his animal. Now what's the emergency?" he asked again.

"Will! I've got the answer. Read this note!"

Will stopped cinching the saddle as he turned to see Tanger and Yann running toward him. Tanger handed him the note and said, "I think that prayer of yours was answered."

Will unfolded the note and felt his whole body flinch as he read the words *cabin, woman, and Charlie*. "Who gave you this, Tanger?"

"An old man I met on Main Street. He said he ran into Charlie and one of the other men on the road. Charlie dropped the note, and the old man picked it up. It's fifteen miles out, and we can be there in plenty of time before dark. I pretty much know the area. I've traveled it enough."

Will looked at both of them and said, "Come on, let's go get my wife." They saddled their horses, picked up their saddlebags at the house as fast as their bodies would allow them to, and headed out.

The Lord had provided the open door, and now it was time for Will and his partners to boldly walk through it.

Chapter Eight

The Measure of a Man

"I'm getting restless with all this waiting. He should have been here by now if he's coming at all," Lester said to Allen.

"He'll be here."

"But what if he isn't smart enough to pick up our trail?"

"Then, Lester, you lost half your money, didn't you. That was the whole purpose of the job; to get him here so that I could see him face to face."

"Lester! Stand guard for a while, will you," Peter hollered.

He took a long drink of water from the bucket that sat on the table with the small ladle before picking up his rifle and heading toward Peter who he found a short distance down the horse path.

"Everything is quiet. I haven't heard a sound," Peter commented.

"I was hoping for some action. Then I'd know the job was done," Lester said.

"You'll get plenty of action soon," Peter said as he headed back up the hill.

కింకింకింకింకింకిం

"Do you think he's really comin' to get ya? Can he find ya? Lester's really smart, ya know," Joey said to Emma.

"He is smart, Joey. But my husband will be here. I believe the Lord is leading him, and you and I are going to be safe. I pray every day for that. We just have to wait," Emma said quietly.

"Don't you get tired of waitin'?"

"Yes, I get tired, and right now I'm very tired."

Joey raised his head to see Allen stand up and move toward them. His right leg was far more painful now than it had been the day before. He repositioned himself to sit more comfortably. He was blessed that the bullet had passed through his calf without hitting the bone. The shot that Peter fired had demonstrated his skill with the six-gun. He could just as easily have killed Joey if he had chosen to.

"I was listening to the both of you. Emma, you'd better hope that he shows up soon because the longer he takes, means the longer you stay," Allen said.

"You plan to kill him, don't you? Because you … you are so full of hate and revenge. You have no kindness at all in you." She covered her face and cried.

Joey wished he could reach out and take hold of him, but Allen was wise enough to keep his distance. Joey also wished he could kill Allen or at least make him wish he was dead. Allen turned and walked back to the chair that sat under the shade tree. It was clear that he had a cold indifference in his heart.

Emma pleaded with God for His grace and forgiveness. Her pain and shame over the past was almost overwhelming to her. Now that she realized the full intent of Allen's plan, her heart felt sick as never before. Knowing that her own sins could possibly cause the death of her husband created a strong anxiety that made her chest ache. She approached the Lord with boldness, confessing that Will had done nothing to bring this situation upon them and that he was innocent. She pleaded with the Lord to protect him.

"What did you say to God?" Joey asked.

"I've done a lot of wrong things in my short life, and now I'm trying to make things right. I was asking God for the strength and courage to do that. My life will never be the same. I can only hope that Will's love for me is as strong as I think it is. I must trust the Lord," she said as she stared straight ahead and wiped her eyes.

"You didn't make us come after you."

"In a way, I did, Joey. It's my past that finally caught up with me. The past that I tried so hard to run from found me."

Joey shook his head and quietly sat thinking.

After wandering around and through the cabin, Peter moseyed on over to Allen and sat down on the ground next to him. "What do you think?" Peter asked.

"More of the same. How I'm going to enjoy seeing his reaction to his not so lily white wife."

"What if he knows all about it? Then all of your thunder will be gone. Did that ever enter your mind?"

"A number of times, Peter, but I know the way she is. She hasn't said a word to him about her past. She painted a different picture of herself, that's what is going to make this whole ordeal, and all its planning, so enjoyable."

"I hope you're right, for your sake, but like I said, he could know all about it," Peter said as he crushed a red ant that was crawling up his arm with his thumb and index finger.

"Can you believe that we're sitting around waiting for a lawman to come to us instead of running from him?" Allen commented.

"Only this one time, brother, only this one time," Peter said from the side of his mouth.

"Allen, do you have any more cloth or a rag I can use for Joey's leg?" Emma asked, interrupting the brothers' conversation.

"No, I don't."

"It's going to get infected if it's not taken care of properly, and I don't want that."

"You're on your own. If he had done his job right, his leg would be fine, wouldn't it?"

"Allen, do you really believe that you are going to get away with this?"

Allen quickly got to his feet and stood before her. His anger boiled over, and he blurted out, "I've waited years for this moment, and I'm going to do it. I'm going to be successful because it's what I want and I—" A deep painful cough stopped his words. He turned and walked back to his chair, his face still red with anger. He removed his handkerchief from his back pocket and wiped his mouth. To his dismay, he saw blood mixed with saliva, a sign that his condition was growing worse.

117

"You've got to learn how to calm down and have some peace. I don't want to be burying you any time soon."

"I really don't care about living a long time. As long as I can take revenge on her, that's all I care about now," Allen said, looking into his older brother's eyes.

"I can't convince you otherwise, can I? I agree with the revenge part, but you're not dead yet, so there's still life to be lived."

"I'm sick. Look at me! I can hardly breath, and I'm spitting up blood again. How can I really live this way, Peter? Tell me. I'm waiting for an answer."

"I don't have an answer." He took a deep breath and exhaled, thinking to himself, *He always was careless.*

"Did you hear that?" Allen asked.

"Yeah, and I saw it. It's a squirrel that just ran up the tree behind you. You're much too jumpy."

෯෯෯෯෯

"I think that's all I can do for your leg right now, Joey. The bleeding has all but stopped, and I don't see any infection yet."

"It's goin' to heal good 'cause I prayed to Jesus just like you told me to. I'm not worryin'."

"Yes, it is going to be fine, because Jesus heard your prayer. You encourage me," Emma said.

She leaned back against the tree and looked up at the sky, which was visible through the branches of the tree. *Lord,* she said, *You have seen fit to work through me to give Joey this new faith. I don't deserve to have Your blessings and Your protection when I look at my life and the results of it. But that's the whole point, Lord; I don't deserve anything. It's all because of Your great love for me. I thought I understood it, but I now see more depth to Your mercy, piety, and love. Thank you, Lord.* She closed her eyes and tried to rest.

෯෯෯෯෯

"I'm sorry, girl. I have no other choice," said Will, stroking her neck in an attempt to calm her.

"We're going to have to put her down, Will. Her leg is definitely broken," Tanger said. "I'll do it for you if you want."

"She's my responsibility; I'll do it. Fortunately she's off the road enough not to block it. She's a good horse, and she belongs to a good friend of mine who was doing me a favor by letting me use her, but I don't have much of a choice," Will said.

Will drew his pistol, pulled back the hammer, and fired one shot, putting her out of her misery. The sound of the shot made the other horses flinch as if they felt it themselves. "I plan on leaving the provisions behind. If there's anything either of you want, take it and make it quick. I have what I need," Will stated.

Tanger grabbed the small cloth bag of dried biscuits and climbed onto Pik. "This might come in handy later," he said. Yann made no comment.

As Will and Yann mounted their horses, Will looked back at the mare he had learned to respect and care for; he felt a bit of stress over what he had just done. *Abe will act like it's a small thing when I explain what happened. But a good horse becomes like a member of the family, and it takes time to get over the loss, also the cost of replacing her will be more than just pocket change,* Will thought.

"I figure it can't be too much longer till we reach the path. I think I know where it's at," Tanger said.

Will nodded his head in acknowledgment and continued to push hard. His mind was full of thoughts. How would they apprehend these men without endangering Emma? While he rode, he prayed for wisdom.

❧❧❧❧❧

Lester wiped the sweat from the front of his neck and the bridge of his nose as he walked back up the path. He felt that walking the path was the best way to keep a good eye on things though he stopped short of the entrance to the main road by a few hundred feet. He didn't want to be seen by the sheriff if he just happened to show up at that moment.

As he reached the top of the path, he saw Peter standing under a tree talking to Allen. Lester said in a loud voice, "Peter, bring me that bucket of drinking water, would you? It's hot over here in the sun."

"Come and get it yourself," said Peter.

"No! I'm not about to let the sheriff sneak up on us. I've worked too hard for this. You can bring it over to me," he said with a tone that showed that he was irritated with Peter's attitude.

Peter took his time carrying the water to Lester. When he reached him, Lester took hold of the handle and quickly drank his fill. "That didn't kill ya, did it?" he said sarcastically.

"I didn't expect it would," Peter said as he turned to walk back to the shade tree, leaving Lester alone to stand watch in the hot sun.

Emma had fallen asleep in the shade of a tree. She had gathered pine needles and a few leaves that were available and made a reasonably comfortable bed. Sleep helped her find a little place of escape from the emotional pain. If someone was to view her as she slept, she could easily be mistaken for a vagabond with hair that hadn't been washed or combed properly in some time and a dirty dress. The silent observer would also see spots of blood on the bottom of the dress from Joey's gunshot wound.

The same squirrel that had startled Allen ran from tree to tree gathering his daily food as the men impatiently waited for what they considered an easy prey. Allen continued to deal with his cough, which was a constant reminder of his mortality. On the other hand, Peter was anxious to get on with the job and return to the woman who he kept back home. Even though Allen was his brother and he was all for this act of revenge, it still had put a strain on their relationship at times.

Allen was so obsessed with finding Emma and her man that life itself was lost track of. They had spent more than two years and a great deal of Peter's money making all of this come together. Allen's reckless and rebellious life had left him with nothing, relying on his brother's willingness to help coupled with his generosity made this act of evil possible. So they sat and watched like cats waiting for a tasty mouse to walk across their path.

With the sun high in the sky along with the bugs biting, irritability was growing in Allen's heart. He spoke harshly to Emma, demanding something to eat. She heard him and opened her eyes, then closed them again. She also said nothing. She was physically and emotionally drained; she had provided them with the best camp food she knew how to. Today she was taking a rest from the hot fire and from scrubbing the iron pot and skillet along with the added tin plates and a mixture of others.

"Did you hear me, Emma? I said, What are we going to have to eat?" Allen repeated.

She sat up, pushing the hair from her face. "Allen, I need to rest. I don't have the strength to cook today. Please let me sleep." She lay down again with her back to them and cried weary tears. *Lord, save me from this. I feel like I'm going to die if Will doesn't come soon. Please, I'm so weak and my heart wants to burst with pain.* Closing her eyes, she tried to sleep.

"Leave her be, Allen. We can feed ourselves. I'll see what there is to eat," Peter said. Allen showed displeasure in his brother's decision by his facial expression.

⇒⇒⇒⇒⇒

"There's the path. See the stones? Ride past a bit, then we'll tie up and go on foot," Will said. They rode about fifty yards and put the horses off the road in a clump of trees. Will was concerned about Emma's safety—this had to be done right. "You both know how I want this done. Think of Emma's safety. All of them up there are probably on edge, and they'll be quick to shoot."

Tanger pulled his Henry from its sheath; he checked his powder and a few other things in his bag. Yann placed his arrow quiver on his back and adjusted it for the fastest pull of an arrow. Will tied the leather strap that hung from the bottom of his holster to his leg. His gun was clean and ready, though he was praying for God's intervention. He wanted a safe arrest with no one harmed. He was hoping for a miracle.

"I couldn't see all the way up the path, but I suspect they have a guard somewhere on it. He's going to have to be taken out first," Tanger said. "I'll go up the right side of the path to take care of the guard." He squatted down and drew in the dirt with his finger, detailing what he knew of the cabin and where he'd position himself once the guard was taken care of. "Yann, about twenty yards from here you can head straight up. That will put you to the left of the cabin in a good position to see pretty much everything," Tanger explained.

"How do you know the layout of the place?" Will asked curiously.

"I ran into the man who built it. He lived in it for two years before abandoning it to move into town." The answer satisfied Will.

"I've given this a lot of thought. I'll give you both ten minutes to settle into position. Then I'll head up just right of the path. I hope to come out behind the cabin." He pointed to the dirt drawing as he said it. "I'm going to holler 'Wyler' to get his attention. Then we'll see how it's all going to play out. You

121

two are in charge of watching my backside," Will said. "OK, let's go. Hey, Tanger, what's the rope for?"

"I might just have to tie somebody up. You never know," Tanger answered.

They walked up the road a short distance before Tanger said, "Yann, this should be about right. Go straight up, and you'll be where you need to be. We need to start together, so wait a minute."

"Remember, you've got ten minutes," Will said.

Once they reached their starting points, Will signaled for them to head up, marking the time with his pocket watch. Will moved in from the road a few yards and sat down. He listened for trouble and prayed for wisdom and strength.

Tanger found the brush and twigs dry and the going slow. He carefully climbed over a downed pine tree. His ten-minute deadline was going to be tight, but that wasn't a big deal. Up ahead and to his left, he saw what he expected to see—a guard watching the path. He took a wide sweep to his right and headed for the large pine that stood near the guard. As he approached the tree, he stepped on and snapped a small branch, catching Lester's immediate attention. Tanger braced himself for this sudden twist in plans. He leaned his rifle against the tree and waited.

Lester moved slowly, with caution. He knew it wasn't a small animal. It had to be a man or some bigger game. But he made the mistake of walking into Tanger's large and powerful left fist, which all but knocked him out. Tanger moved quickly, taking an old piece of red flannel along with a leather tie from his bag and gagging his mouth. He tied his hands and feet behind him; then he used the remaining rope to tie him to the tree. Lester was not going anywhere.

With the feeling of a job well done, he moved up the hill. He found a mostly decayed log that at one time was a proud mature tree before it was put to rest. He placed his rifle barrel across the log and laid himself down behind it. He was in a good position. He had come in above them, so he could clearly see the two remaining men, but he couldn't see Emma. He checked his sights, pulled back the hammer, and waited for Will.

Tanger didn't have to wait long. Will reached the cabin sooner than he had planned, or maybe it was the stress that made the time disappear. He moved quickly, keeping himself low as he ran over the clearing to the side of the cabin the distance of about twenty yards. He peeked in the side window of the cabin and found it empty. He sensed a musty smell coming from the window that made his nose tingle. Will took a few deep breaths, asked the Lord for help, and then said, "Wyler … !"

Peter jumped to his feet and said, "He's here. Get up, Allen!"

Emma opened her sleeping eyes at the sound of Will's voice, causing her entire body to flinch. He was here! She covered her mouth so as not to scream, and she lay as if she were lifeless. She knew enough not to draw Will's attention away from what was most important and that was to stop the Hoffmans. She repositioned herself on the opposite side of the tree where she felt safer and out of sight. She continued to lay motionlessly as if she were a fawn hiding from harm.

"So you made it, Jacobs. For a while I had my doubts," Peter said sarcastically.

"No you didn't. You've been expecting me. You have my wife!"

"By the way, the name's not Wyler. It's Peter Hoffman and my brother Allen here. Have you ever heard the name before, Jacobs?"

"No, your name means nothing to me."

"It will! Why don't you step out into the open so we can see each other face to face. I always like to see my enemies," Allen challenged.

Before stepping out, Will checked his gun and slipped it back into its holster. He walked straight toward the brothers, stopping approximately twenty feet in front of them. He stood there without saying a word, but his silence spoke loudly, along with his steady unflinching eyes. He then spoke. "You were going to tell me why I should know you."

"Yea, my brother has something to say to you that I think you'll find very interesting. I know I did at first," Peter replied.

"Jacobs, I've waited a long time for this moment. To be precise, I waited years to say this to you. Your sweet little Emma and I go back a long ways. Did she ever tell you that she ran away from home at fifteen to be with me, an older man of twenty-five? Or that we made our living by robbing folks of their jewels and other fine things like money, guns, even food, and clothing, at times? I wouldn't expect her to still like the whiskey and gin, seeing that she has found Jesus these days.

"But we had some real high times together, her and I. She was real sweet on me back then, but she ran off and left me just before we were caught. Then I ended up in prison to almost rot in that dark cell alone. Do you think I've liked carrying this sickness and limp with me these past years, Jacobs? Well, I don't, I don't.

"And don't think that I sat around dreaming all this up or that I'm out of my mind? Tell me, Jacobs, does she still have that cute little mole on her left shoulder?" He used his right index finger to point out the exact spot he was referring to. "We were lovers and outlaws for almost two years. Then she ran off with a fine ruby necklace and matching earrings, along with some diamonds she kept in the saddlebags. She must have sold them to make her new start.

"I can tell by the look on your face that she painted a pretty picture of herself; that this is the first you've heard about all of this. Did she every mention her folks or her older sister? Her folks would have paid me to take her off their hands if they knew she was running off with me. And her sister ran off and was never heard from again," Allen finished his speech with a coughing spell.

"So what's the purpose of all this? Did you two go through all this trouble to tell me that my wife's not perfect and that she did a few things wrong in her past. I'm not buying that," he said.

"Actually, we went through all of this so I could have the pleasure of killing you, because if I can't have her neither can you."

Through the corner of his eye, Will could see a man standing up. He used this opportunity to try to distract Hoffman for a moment.

"Hoffman, who's that behind you, moving toward you?"

"Nice try, but it's only the half-wit Joey," Allen said.

"I've come here for my wife. Now let me see her."

"And how are you going to leave with her, seeing that you walked in here alone? I'd be watchin' my backside if I were you. And about seeing Emma, she's here, and you know she is or you wouldn't have walked in here and put your life on the line," Allen stated.

"I'm not worried about my backside. The man you had guarding the path, the one you thought you could rely on, has already been taken out of the way." Will spoke from hope and trust in Tanger, but not from certainty. He needed them to think he was in complete control, that no details had slipped through the cracks.

Will took a few steps forward and said, "Drop your guns. I don't want to shoot the two of you today. I want this to be peaceful."

"Pretty confident, aren't you, Jacobs?"

Will nodded his head and said, "Yes I am, and now you've been warned."

This was not working out the way Allen had planed or dreamed it would. He started to become fearful. He raised his rifle and proceeded to point it in Will's direction. "I've waited too long and for too many years to have you spoil my plans. I'm going to have my revenge, and I'm going to have it now!" But before Allen could pull the trigger, he began to shake all over from another coughing spell—the cough that haunted him day and night. He took a half dozen steps backward and fell down on the ground unable to move.

Tanger decided it was time to make his move. He squeezed off a shot, putting a hole in the water bucket large enough to poke your thumb through.

Will dove to the ground, drawing his gun on the way down. He took aim at Peter without firing. To his surprise, Peter fell forward onto his knees, holding the back of his head, and then he fell on his right side, still grasping his head and moaning in pain. Will quickly got to his feet and ran over to Peter. He saw blood coming from the back of his head, but he had no idea why. But he didn't waste any time pulling a pair of handcuffs from his back pocket, cuffing Peter's hands behind his back, and then proceeding to do the same to Allen.

Allen looked on silently in disbelief. His plans of revenge had been shattered by the man he hated most. The reason for his hate was simple—he was jealous and filled with envy for what he didn't have and never could have: another man's life of love, contentment, and Emma. It was his own heart that robbed him of his own life.

Will looked up from his knees and caught a view of the back of Emma's head. He jumped up and ran to her. She was lying on her side rolled up in a ball. Will knelt down beside her—his heart broke at the sight of her. "Emma, it's me, Will. You're safe now. We're going home." She raised her head, put out her arms, and cried. "Will, Will, I'm sorry for putting you through this. It's my past that's caused all of this. I love you. Please forgive me; please forgive me," she said through her tears.

Will lifted her up and held her tight. It was good to hold her. He kissed her a number of times and then said, "Honey, the past is over. That was all before we met. I love you very much. Thinking about not finding you and living without you was too much for me. I would have died trying to find you." He held her so tight he thought he might break her, but she didn't complain.

125

"Can you walk?"

"Yes."

Will helped Emma to her feet, and as they stepped around the tree, they saw Joey standing with the aid of a makeshift crutch while Yann watched over the Hoffmans.

"Where's Tanger?"

"I don't know. I haven't seen him yet. He should be coming soon, I'd think."

"I want to get them loaded up and get back to Yreka before dark, Yann. I think we can make it if we head out soon," Will said.

Will got Emma a drink of water and then went searching for Tanger. He walked over to the path and heard the sound of twigs breaking, so he called out, "Tanger, is that you?"

"Yeah, it's me, Will. I got a little something for you. I'll be right there."

"I want to get to Yreka before dark."

Appearing from the woods with his captive in tow, Tanger said, "Look what I found. He was their guard, but not the smartest one I've ever seen. He was easy to take." Lester's hands were still tied and his mouth still gagged.

"Let's take the gag out of his mouth so he can breathe better," Will said as he untied it. "So you must be Lester, now tell me, where's Charlie?"

After the gag was removed, Lester spit and said, "Charlie's dead; he shot himself."

Will took the last pair of handcuffs from his pocket and handed them to Tanger. "I want these on him," he said. He walked back up the short hill to Emma. He knelt down before her on one knee. She put her arms around his neck and said, "Will, I need to leave. I can't look at these men anymore. I want to go now, please."

"Show me what horse you've been riding, and we'll go." He turned to Tanger who was just approaching and said to him, "We're going to ride ahead of you back to town. I'm going to leave the men with you. Take them to the sheriff's office. He said he'd have room to lock them up. I'll see you in town later."

"What do I do with this one?" Tanger asked.

"That's Joey," Emma said. "He's become my friend, and he's been good to me. Peter shot him in the leg for trying to protect me. He really isn't one of them, and I don't want him arrested. He's going to need to see a doctor though."

"I want you to take her to my ma's house. You can stay as long as you need. We'll sleep at the stable like before. And don't worry about our prisoners, we'll take good care of 'em," Tanger said.

"Thanks, Tanger. See ya in town later," Will replied as he and Emma walked toward the horses.

"That saddle and this horse, Will," Emma pointed out. He quickly saddled the horse and helped her up.

After she was settled, he looked up at her and said, "I thank God that you're all right, and that I've found you. I love you."

She ran her fingers through his hair. "I love you, too."

He took the reins of her horse and led the way down the path toward Bella. Max saw Will and came running to him. He was impressed once again that at Tanger's command Max would be so obedient. He rubbed the top of Max's head and said, "You're a good boy. I want you to stay here and wait for Tanger."

He untied and mounted Bella, moving close to Emma. Smiling, he said, "I'd rather have you ride double with me, but I know that won't work, so a kiss will have to do." After receiving his reward, they took off for Yreka.

❧❧❧❧❧❧

"I think we're ready, Yann," Tanger said. He had tied all three men together at the waist with enough room between each other to walk behind the horses as they made their way to the main road and the other horses. They had walked a short distance when Peter said, "Tell me, genius, how are we going to ride with our hands cuffed behind our backs?"

Tanger knew the question was directed toward him. He didn't answer at first; he just continued to ride. As they reached their own horses, they dismounted. Max sized up the strangers and decided that an inspection by sniffing everyone was needed. "I've got the answer to your question, Hoffman. If you can get your hands around the front of you, that's all right with me."

Tanger stepped over to them and removed the rope from their waists. Peter quickly lay down on his back and worked his cuffed hands under his legs to the backside of his knees. He then brought his knees to his chest and worked the cuffs past his boots. He was now free enough to straighten his hat, wipe the sweat from his face, but mostly to hold onto the saddle horn for better balance. Allen Hoffman and Lester didn't meet with the same success, so Tanger redid their handcuffs in front of them. He had fifteen miles to ride before dark! So he became pushy.

These men were going to be difficult, and Tanger knew it. There was Allen with his hate for anything or anyone that didn't follow his plans. Now Peter had a slightly different twist to his personality—he had to be in control, the toughest one on the top of the heap, and he would not settle for less. Lester had a simple philosophy—dream big and lie, cheat, and steal to fulfill your dreams.

Knowing that he was going to have to be real hard on them to keep them from escaping, Tanger said, "Don't think that I won't tie you belly-down to your horse if you give me any trouble or that if you try to run off that I won't shoot you. I hope you're listening because I'm very serious! Joey, you take the reins to Allen's horse; Yann, you get Lester, and I'll take Peter, the mouthy one."

He really wished he had a wagon to put them all in. That would be a much safer way to transport the prisoners. He'd have to talk it over with Will. Perhaps Monty might have one that could be borrowed for a time, or it may cost him some unpaid labor seeing the type of businessman Monty was.

They rode off in a trot with Tanger in the lead. He would hold that pace for as long as possible seeing that he needed to cover this ground before dark. After a time the trotting came to an end, for even the best-conditioned horse couldn't keep up the pace that Tanger was trying to hold. But he had closed some of the gap between themselves and Yreka.

"I need medical care. My head is splitting," Peter blurted out.

Joey filled in the missing piece of the puzzle as to the cause for Peter's headache. "I hit you real good with that rock, didn't I? I picked it up from the creek before I got to the cabin. It was made for throwin'. It was just like an egg. When I was a boy, I would throw little rocks through knotholes in trees, so you were an easy target."

"Think of that! An outlaw with a gun made helpless with a rock thrown by a man who doesn't carry a gun. Joey, you did a good job. Hey, Peter, you should thank him. He probably saved your life today, because you're not fast enough to draw on Will. A knot on the head is better than a bullet. I'll have someone look at you when you're safely locked up," Tanger said.

ॐॐॐॐॐॐ

The sun was quickly sliding out of sight as Will knocked on Cora's front door. The time it took for the door to open seemed like a small eternity. Cora stood in the open doorway with a surprised look on her face, turning and saying, "Leah, it's the sheriff and his wife. They're back. He found her! Come in, come in. Please, sit down." She led the way into the dining room.

Leah walked in and said, "Hi, I'm Leah. It's nice to meet you. You must be Emma? I'm thankful they found you. You must be hungry! Would you also like some tea, my dear?"

"Yes, I would, please," Emma responded.

"Sit down with them, Leah. I'll get everything," Cora said.

"It must have been a horrifying experience these many weeks. Please accept my deep sympathy. If you need anything at all, please ask. I'd feel honored to help, Emma."

Cora came in a few minutes later and set cups and a teapot on the table and returned to the kitchen without a word passing her lips.

"Thank you. It's so nice to sit and to be in your home. I don't have all the words that my heart is feeling. I will never forget your kindness toward me, Leah."

"I have a bath just off the kitchen with a privacy curtain. It's wonderful! My husband, Robert, just finished building it two weeks ago, and I've washed my whole body three times already. It's so refreshing."

"I'd love that. I've hardly washed since this all happened, but it will be cold like the river, won't it?"

"No, Emma. I heat water on the stove. I'll show you after you eat. You'll be spoiled and never want to use the river again. If you'll excuse me, I'm going to go check on Cora. Sometimes she's slow about things."

Emma took Will's hand in hers and asked, "How did you hurt your mouth and face? And I see that your front tooth is broken"

"At Fort Reading two men jumped me and beat me badly. It happened by surprise. I couldn't stop them." He paused and looked into her eyes. "Emma, I would have taken a dozen beatings to find you and bring you back home."

"This is all my fault. My past has suddenly caused you and Loretta so

129

much pain. Please forgive me for bringing all of this on you. I have a lot of explaining to do, but right here is not the place."

"When you're ready to talk, I'll be more than ready to listen," he said.

"I love you more than ever before. You deserve an answer to all that has happened. You must have some questions and maybe a few doubts. I want you to understand everything."

"Here's your dinner. I hope you enjoy it," Leah said as she placed two heaping plates of food before them. "I'm going to go through my dresses. I must have one that will fit you, Emma, and I'm going to start filling the bath," Leah stated before she left the room.

Will and Emma had a heartfelt prayer before starting their meal. Suddenly Emma's eyes filled with tears that rolled down her cheeks. *You are so loving to me, Jesus. Thank you for your kindness and for guiding Will to me*, she prayed in her head.

"Why the tears, honey?" Will asked.

She put down her fork and wrapped her arms around his neck. "I'm overwhelmed with God's love for me and your love and now their kindness to me. I'm safe with you and away from those men, and we can go home and see Loretta. I miss her so much; I need to hold her. There were times when I thought I was going to die or that we both would die and leave Loretta alone. I'm sorry for not telling you the truth about my past, about the kind of girl I was. I was afraid that you wouldn't want someone like me. I thought I might lose you because I fell in love with you so quickly." She started sobbing.

"Emma, my life wasn't perfect either. I had girlfriends, and I drank a lot of whiskey. I was hateful and more. There's things I've never told you. Jesus used you to reach me, to open my blind eyes to a new world that I never dreamed of before. I owe you so much. Please understand that the past is over, and what happened before you met me doesn't matter. You and Loretta are gifts from God, and I love you very much."

She released her hold on his neck and looked into his blue eyes. She smiled, lightly kissed him, and moved her plate and chair closer beside him. "You're a wonderful man, Will. Thank you for what you just said. It gives me strength."

"We should eat some of this food before it gets cold, and your bath is going to be ready in a bit," he said caringly. They sat quietly for a few moments, and she reveled in the sense of security she felt with him by her side—it was a good feeling.

A few minutes later the front door opened, and Tanger entered. "Will, we made it all right, but I need to talk to you about a few things."

"I don't think you need to hear any of this, honey. Why don't you check on how the bath is coming, and I'll talk to Tanger."

"OK, I'll do that," she said as she got up and headed for the kitchen.

Tanger was waiting in the tiny sitting room off the foyer. He looked up as Will entered. "I'm glad you made it back safely," Will said. "What's on your mind?"

Tanger leaned forward in his chair and said, "We need a wagon. Doing this on horseback could spell trouble, and we need money. I had to get a doctor to look at Peter's head, and there's the food too."

"I know. I've been hoping that one of them has a bounty on them. I do have some money, and Yann told me we could use his money from the sale of the horse if we needed to. You must know someone that you can borrow a wagon from."

"I plan to check on a wagon in the morning. Maybe I can get it for free. Yann and Joey are watching the men. We're doing it in shifts since we figured you'd want time with your wife."

"Did the marshall say anything about Yann watching the men and him being Chinese?"

"No, not a word."

"I'm surprised," Will said. "But that's good. Now, I have a big thing to ask of you, Tanger."

"What's that?"

"I want to leave ahead of you. I don't think it would be healthy for Emma to have to spend any more time with the prisoners. She needs to be free of them."

"That makes sense. I'll take charge of getting them back to Stone Ridge. Enjoy your wife, brother. I give you my word that these men won't escape. We'll be in Stone Ridge as soon as we can."

"Thanks for everything. I'm going to talk to the marshall before we leave in the morning. By the way, are you hungry? There's food on the table if you want. I'm going to check on Emma."

"Yeah, I am," Tanger said, and they both went their separate ways.

Will made his way toward the kitchen where Leah had said the bath was. The room was quiet except for the soft sound of splashing water. "Emma, how are you doing?" Will asked through the curtain

"Just fine, dear. I think the first eight layers of dirt are gone. There's just a few left, and I'll be clean. Can I have a bath like this at home?"

"I can try to get one. I wanted to let you know that we're leaving in the morning ahead of Tanger and the prisoners. We're going on horseback so that we can get home as fast as possible."

Will continued, "It's getting late and tomorrow will come soon. We should turn in, honey. I want to leave early in the morning."

"Give me just a few minutes more. Could you please check with Leah about the clothes?" she asked.

Will found Leah in the sitting room with an armful of blankets for their makeshift beds. "Will, you can sleep on the floor. I'm putting Emma here on the loveseat."

"That's fine, thank you. Emma needs the clothes you offered. She's ready to get out of the bath," Will said. "By the way, we want to leave early in the morning if we can."

Leah nodded her head and said, "I'll be up to see you off and get you some breakfast. I'm done here. I'll get the clothes for Emma."

"Where's Robert?"

"Working, I hope. He does what he pleases most of the time. He'll be home when he gets here," she said as she walked into the next room.

He removed his boots and gun, lay down on his bedroll, and was almost asleep when he felt Emma kiss him on the cheek. "You need a bath and shave, my dear husband," she said as she lay down and covered herself with one of the blankets. She reached down and placed her hand on his chest, and they both slipped into a contented sleep.

ớ◦ớ◦ớ◦ớ◦ớ◦

Emma was awakened by the sound of pots and pans from the kitchen. The ladies were already busy with their morning responsibilities. She sat up and rubbed her right foot over Will's chest. He opened his eyes and quickly took hold of her foot and began to tickle it. It was good to have life starting to return to normal, which included enjoying simple things with her husband. "That's enough of that," she said with a laugh. She stood up, grabbed her clothes, and ran off to find somewhere to dress. Will got up, too, and after putting on his little bit of gear, he told Emma that he was headed to the marshall's office.

Things were going smoothly. The marshall was in, and so was Joey. Joey caught Will's eye and said, "Tanger and Yann went to get a wagon. They said they'd be back when they got one."

After settling up business with the marshall, Will went to talk to Lester. He unlocked the door that separated the office from the cell. As he entered, they all looked up. Allen was still coughing, and Lester said nothing—he was still nursing a sore jaw. It was Peter who spoke, "Well, look who it is, the hero."

"I'm not here to talk to you, so keep your mouth shut. Lester, answer me just one question, how did you know when I'd be out of town so you could take my wife that day?"

"What if I don't tell ya, sheriff?"

"Well, Lester, I won't get my answer, and you'll still hang. The penalty for kidnapping is hanging, and on top of that, I can charge you with attempted murder of a lawman."

He sat quietly for a minute or so before answering. "I'll tell ya just so you can see that you can't trust anybody. When you get back home go ask your deputy, Henry, how I knew everything. He would have sold me the whole town if I had the cash." He put his head back and laughed loudly.

Now the pieces fit together. Will could clearly see this wasn't over yet. Henry, his own deputy, had turned on him. As he started to leave, Lester said, "Are you happy now, sheriff, that you got your answer?"

Will didn't respond. Instead, he closed the inner office door behind him and turned to address the marshall. "Tanger should be in soon to take them off your hands. I'm riding out ahead of them. Thanks for everything you've done to help."

"It's the least I could do for another lawman, and I won't forget to check on the bounty for you. Take care, and remember to watch your backside." They shook hands and Will left.

As he walked out, he thought, *I can't let Emma know about Henry, about the evil thing he has done. The case had just become much more complicated.*

Emma was sitting on the porch waiting for him. As he approached the house, she stood up and hugged him. "I've packed the few things we have. Cora and

Leah gave us enough food for a two-day ride. I'm ready to go, my dear."

"So am I. Let's say goodbye and then drop by the stable to see if Tanger or Yann is there."

Will reached for the doorknob but the door opened before he could turn the handle, revealing both ladies standing in the doorway. "We know you have to go and that you're in a hurry, so we came to say a quick goodbye. It was so nice to have you stay with us. Please come back, if you can." They all hugged, and Will and Emma mounted their horses and rode toward the stable, but when they arrived, they found only Harry sitting in his old chair in front of the door.

"Have you seen Tanger today?"

"Just for a minute or so. Him and the Chinaman took off. They're lookin' for a wagon. That's all I can tell ya."

"When you see him, tell him that Will and his wife left for home."

"That would be Stone Ridge, right?"

"Yes, take care," Will said, and they turned their horses toward home.

Chapter Nine

The Trail Home

"We should see the fort soon, it's just a mile or so on the left," encouraged Will.

"Good, we need a rest," Emma responded. They had pushed hard since leaving Yreka, since they were trying to make it to Fort Reading in two days. The sky had been clear for days now, which gave the sun the privilege of shining brighter and stronger. This also pleased the biting flies that dogged them all the way. In spite of all of this, Emma had joy—she was free. She now understood more deeply the meaning of the word. She was on her way home, which added joy upon joy to her heart.

"This is it, Emma, our place of rest for the night." She looked forward to a meal and a good night's sleep. She also looked forward to meeting Kate and her son. Will had told her about the beating he had received and the irreplaceable help that Kate had given him. The long hours on the trail were spent in pouring out their hearts to each other. Emma filled in all the gaps in here life that the Hoffman brothers had left out. She spoke of her childhood and the abuse that her father had heaped upon her and her sister. She described the many times her father would beat her mother, sometimes to the edge of life before he would stop, before the drunken beast in him was finished. If her sister was not available, it then became Emma's turn for the beatings, which left few physical scars but many emotional ones.

The fort was less crowded this time. As they maneuvered around a wagon in front of a row of buildings, Will stopped a soldier passing by on foot and asked directions to the infirmary. He dismounted before receiving an answer; it felt good to stand on the ground. The soldier stopped and placed his right hand on his hip and said, "If it was a snake, it would have bit you." He pointed to the sign above Will's head and continued on his way, shaking his head.

"Thanks for the help," he said as he tied up the horses and helped Emma down. "Kate should be here. It will be a lot more comfortable staying with her than on the ground. Come on, I'll introduce you," he said. He knocked on the door, but there was no answer, so he pulled the latch and walked in. The room was dark except for a small lamp that was left burning on the table across the room. The infirmary was void of a window, cheating its occupants of any natural light, so the lamp was the only light in the room.

"Kate! It's Will Jacobs. I'm back with Emma. Are you here?" he called out.

"Maybe Kate and the doctor are so good that everyone is healthy," Emma said with a laugh.

"In this place that would be a miracle, my dear."

At that moment Kate and Clay entered through the open door. Kate's eyes grew huge with excitement when she realized who was standing in front of her. "Will, you're back! And you must be Emma. Thank God you're safe!" Stepping forward she hugged them both, and in the dim light, she looked Emma over the best she could. She then said, "I feel like I already know you. Will talked a great deal about you as he healed. You're going to stay a few days with us and rest, aren't you? That will give Emma and I time to get acquainted."

"We can only stay the night. We want to get home to our little girl."

"I understand. Well, let's get you settled. You can stay with me."

"We'd appreciate that, Kate," Will said.

Kate motioned with her right hand and led the way down the steps to the right. As they walked she asked how Eric was doing and where he was.

"He's on his way. Yann is also with him. They're taking care of the three prisoners. They should be here in a day or two."

"Did you say Yann is with him?"

"Yeah, he joined back up with us, but that is a story in itself. When they get here, ask him what happened. You'll be amazed. Because of it all he now believes in the Lord."

"Here's my little abode," Kate said.

Clay, who had been quiet, suddenly interjected, "I got a cat. A soldier gave him to me, and his name is Rusty. I bet you'll like him. I do."

"I bet you're right, Clay," Will answered.

As they entered the front room, Emma saw a neat and comfortable little place. It held a table and three chairs. The table was set with a cream colored plate with light pink roses atop a white cotton tablecloth. A shelf, which held half a dozen cups, hung from the wall behind the table. A hard-to-find potbelly stove sat proudly to the left of the doorway which led to a second smaller room.

"I'm going to take care of the horses while there's still enough light," Will said.

"Please don't be gone long."

"I'll make it quick, Emma," he replied as he gently touched her right hand.

"Ma, can I go with him?" Clay asked.

"Yes, just mind yourself," she stated.

"Thanks, Ma," he said with a slam of the door as he ran to catch up to Will.

Kate pointed to one of the chairs and said, "Sit down, please. I'm going to put water on for tea, would you like some?"

"Yes, I would love some," Emma answered.

There was a silence between them as Kate went about her business of starting a fire and filling the teapot. Emma thought of the distance left to ride before reaching home and considered the possibility of saddle sores. She quickly sent up a prayer of protection against them.

Kate spoke first as she sat down. "I'm saving the rest of the biscuits for supper, but we can enjoy a few now with our tea. I made vegetable soup this morning from a dry mix I have. I'm sorry I don't have more to offer you. I had no idea when you'd be arriving."

"Please don't be sorry. What you have is more than enough, Kate. The Lord has allowed me to learn some very important lessons through all that has happened. For one, I've learned to be content with what I have, and second, I feel like the child in me has grown up. That little girl who was running away from herself has finally come home. I'm no longer running. Also, I couldn't ask for a more loving husband. I thank God that he never stopped looking for me. He's a strong man, and I receive a lot of strength from him. I love him more now than ever. Oh, I'm sorry. Maybe I've said too much since we've just met."

"Bless you, Emma. You're thankful even with all the pain. I pray that you get home to Loretta soon. Will told me about her. She sounds so sweet."

"That's why we're leaving early in the morning."

"After breakfast, I hope."

"Yes, after breakfast. Will gets grumpy on an empty stomach."

"Don't most men," Kate said with a laugh.

The boiling water made itself known by commanding their attention. Kate obeyed by jumping up and removed it from the stove. She poured the steaming concoction into the waiting cups. The aroma floated up to Emma's nose—she enjoyed its freshness and how it filled her senses. She was starting to feel as if the pieces of her life were once again fitting into place. It was a peaceful moment that she was thankful for.

"I wonder how our men are doing," Emma said.

"The longer they take, the longer we can visit. Clay needs time with a good man like yours. His Father died when he was barely four, which has left an empty spot in his heart that I haven't been able to fill. Eric is the first man since his father that he could get close to, and Will has also helped greatly."

"Is Eric, Tanger's first name?" Emma asked.

"Yup."

"I didn't know that. Will told me how they met and how close they became in a short time. He also hinted that Tanger has feelings for you and that he plans to act upon them, but he didn't say that Tanger was Eric."

"Yes, he is, and I have his promise that he's coming back. I believe him to be honest. He'll be here soon I hope," she said with excitement in her voice. She quickly stood to her feet and moved toward the stove. She bent down and picked up a medium-sized cast iron pot. It had been resting on top of a footstool to the left of the stove. She maneuvered it next to the teapot on top of the stove.

"The sun is going down. Do you have candles or a lamp? I can light whichever you have."

"Yes, the lamp is right behind you on the floor. Please feel free to light it."

The door opened and then closed with its ritualistic slamming. "Ma, we bedded down the horses, and Will let me ride Bella to the stable. After we were done, he told me to come back here because he went to see the lieutenant."

"I'm glad you had a good time, son. From now on I want you to call him 'Mr. Will' out of respect, seeing that he's a grown man and a sheriff, too. Did he say how long he'd be gone?" Kate asked.

"No, Ma, he just told me to go back home and stay there, that's all."

"Mr. Will must have known that dinner will be ready soon. Would you take the lamp from Mrs. Jacobs and hang it up please." Clay took one of the chairs and moved it to the center of the room where a hook was attached to a chain hung from the ceiling. He placed the handle of the lamp on the hook. "Is there anything else you want, Ma?"

"You can bring in some more wood and put it next to the stove."

He left the chair in the middle of the room and headed outside.

๑๑๑๑๑๑

"Come in!" Will heard through the closed door. The lieutenant was at his desk when he eyed Will. "You made it back in one piece! Congratulations, sheriff. Tell me, how's your wife? Good, I hope, and how about that Tanger? Is he with you?"

"Yes and no," Will said as he reached out to shake the lieutenant's hand. "My wife held up pretty good. She's with Kate right now. Tanger has the three men. He's behind us a day or two. He'll need room in the stockade when he arrives. Emma and I are riding ahead of him. We plan to leave in the morning. Would you take down these names?"

The lieutenant grabbed a pen and a small piece of paper and said, "Go ahead."

"Peter and Allen Hoffman—those two are the leaders. Lester—I don't have a last name on him yet. There was Charlie Woodman, but he's dead. He shot himself the day before we caught up with them. Make sure you alert your guards that these men are dangerous."

"Thanks for the warning," he said as he gave Will a quick look and commented, "You look like you're healing pretty well. I still remember seeing you flat on your back looking like you had been drug behind a horse."

"Yes, lieutenant, I am healing well. That's what good food and care, mixed with a lot of God's blessings will do for a man."

"My mother is a real churchgoer, but for me, I can't tell if it works or not. Anyway, do you have any interest in seeing Perkins and the other man? I can walk over with you if you do."

"No, they caused me enough trouble. I don't need to be reminded of it, but thanks for asking anyway. Lieutenant, I have appreciated all the help you've provided. Take care."

"Likewise, Will, likewise."

As the door shut behind him, Will tipped his head back and looked up. The night sky was clear, and the stars were starting to glow brightly. He took in the beauty before him and said out loud, "Lord, thank you for all of this. Thank you for giving Emma back to me. I will never forget this, and I say this from my heart." His thoughts were broken by the sound of two soldiers passing by just a short distance from him. He started back to Kate's, hoping that some food would be ready. He was hungry.

Emma turned her head toward the door in hopes that it was Will that had made the noise. She wasn't disappointed. "Hi, dear, come in and sit down. We just started a few minutes ago. It's vegetable soup with biscuits. We already said the blessing."

Will sat down between Clay and Emma and then took a large bite of his biscuit, washing it down with a spoonful of soup.

"All the business is taken care of. In the morning I just have to saddle the horses and fix the gear. Oh no, I left all the gear in the stable! That was foolish of me. I was more concerned with seeing the lieutenant than the gear."

"Finish your supper first. I'm sure it will be safe until then," Emma remarked.

"Mr. Will?"

"What is it, Clay?"

"Can I help you saddle up the horses in the mornin'?"

"I don't see why not, and you can go get the gear with me after supper."

"Thanks!" Will reached over and rubbed the top of his head, messing up his hair a little more than it already was. Before putting his hand down, he picked up a second biscuit and dipped it into his soup.

"Do you have any idea where you would like to settle down?" Emma asked Kate.

"Not here at the fort, that I know. More than likely it will involve a certain man I intend to court," she answered.

"Stone Ridge is a nice town. I'd love to have you come and stay. It has good people there, and we have a fine group of believers. Please consider it."

"I will give it some thought, Emma."

"This is a fine meal, Kate. Thank you," Will said.

"I'm glad you are enjoying it," Kate replied.

After Will had finished two large bowls of soup and more than his share of biscuits, he pushed his bowl toward the center of the table and said, "Clay and I are going to head over to the stable and get the gear. We'll be back soon."

"Hurry back. I'd like to get to sleep early," Emma stated.

"Promise," Will said.

The night air was warm and the moon almost full. "Do you like the stars, Clay?"

"Yeah, I really like shooting stars. They go so fast."

"The heavens are a wonder to me. The Bible says that God made them all."

As they entered the stable, a young soldier eyed them and said, "Mister, is that your gear over there?"

"Yeah it is. I was just coming to get it."

"It's a good way to lose it, mister."

"You're right, thanks for watching it. What's your name, soldier?"

"Johnny Farrington."

"Would you mind helping me carry the gear to where I'm staying?"

"No, not at all mister."

"Where are you stayin?"

"With Kate; she's the nurse. You can follow me," he said, picking up a saddlebag and placing it over his shoulder. He then grabbed the two saddles, one for each hand, and started out.

As they approached Kate's, Clay opened the door wide. They set the gear in the middle of the floor. "I see you found a good man to help. How are you, Johnny?"

"I'm fine, Miss Kate."

"Will, Johnny Farrington is known for his honesty and hard work. And he is one of the few here who has faith in our Lord."

"Farrington, that's an impressive report. I hope people can say that of me."

He nodded his head "yes" and asked, "Who are you, mister?"

"I'm Will Jacobs, the sheriff of Stone Ridge, south of here. Thanks for all your help. It was good of you. It's getting late, and I think we need to get some sleep. Take care of yourself, and thanks again."

"I sure will," Johnny said as he left.

Will sorted out the gear as Emma assembled the makeshift bed on the floor. When all was ready, good nights were said and with lamps out Will and Emma found themselves sharing thoughts and a prayer before falling asleep.

ลลลลล

The sky was a pleasant blue, and the grounds were alive with horses, equipment, and approximately two dozen men. They were making ready to ride north for a few days, a soldier told Will as he saddled the horses. It appeared to be more than a few days' ride, Will thought, as he noticed a supply wagon roll by the stable. He finished saddling the horses and led them out past the confusion of the not-so-assembled soldiers. Bella whinnied to a horse nearest her and received a hearty response in return, which made her prance a bit.

As Will approached Kate's place, he found the women waiting outside the door with the remaining gear. "Thanks for getting things ready," he said.

"I thought it would make it easier for you, Mr. Jacobs," Emma said, smiling her attractive smile, which made Will feel warm inside. He smiled back and started loading their things.

"How many miles do you think we can ride today?" she asked as she helped with the task at hand.

"I was hoping for about forty, but that might be a dream. I'd say twenty-five anyway."

She finished tying the last of the goods to her horse, gave a thankful hug to Kate, and pulled herself up into the saddle.

"Thanks again, Kate, for all your hospitality. Say hi to the men when they arrive, and stay away from the prisoners. We hope to see you in Stone Ridge soon," Will said from the saddle.

"I pray you two have a safe trip," Kate said as she waved goodbye.

ลลลลล

Will and Emma had spent many long days on the road, but they were now within minutes of their roots. Their days had been a mix of weariness and heat with just enough rain to make one wet and uncomfortable. But there had been an upside to the trip—the beauty of the hills, meadows, birds, and the undeniable majesty of Mount Shasta with its open meadows at its base.

"Emma, look, there's George Brewster's place! We are home, my dear." Brewster owned a shack on the outer edge of town. He was a middle-aged man who was rarely seen. Will could never figure him out. As they passed the short road that led to their home, Main Street made its appearance. Like a cup without a bottom, her emotions drained from her, filling her eyes with tears that flowed down her face. Will took notice of her feelings and lightly touched her shoulder. He then proceeded to take the reins from her, leading the horse.

Some people waved while others didn't take notice. Abe's place was their first stop. Will dismounted and helped Emma down, taking her hand as they entered the store. Abe was stocking shelves when he looked up and saw them. He almost tripped getting to his feet. "Emma, Will, you're back! Elizabeth come quick, they're back!" he shouted.

"Hi," Will managed to say before Abe wrapped them in a bear hug.

Elizabeth had heard Abe's voice and went to the backyard to get Loretta. They soon emerged from behind the counter. As soon as Loretta saw Emma, she ran to her with her arms open wide. "Mommy, Mommy, you're back," she cried.

Elizabeth couldn't hold back the tears. They ran down her cheeks as she watched the most beautiful reunion of the Jacobs family. With the ladies and Loretta on their way upstairs to talk, share, and cry, Will asked Abe, "What condition is the town in?"

"It's not good. Henry rode out three nights ago. No one has seen him since, and I don't know if he's coming back."

"Who's in charge then?"

"Deputy Radcliff."

"Otis Radcliff?"

"Yeah, Henry hired him."

"Where's Buckley?" Will asked next.

"He's been sick almost a month now, but there's one more thing you need to know."

"What's that."

"It's about the Atkin brothers, Tim and Roy. They've been causing a lot of trouble with their drinking and fighting, and some of the shop owners are complaining about things missing. They showed up four weeks ago. Henry couldn't handle them, neither can Radcliff. I think they're from Green Valley."

"I should have never given Henry the job to begin with. Keep this to yourself, Abe, but I found out that Henry was in on the kidnapping. I was hoping to lock him up when the prisoners got here. Things change quickly, don't they? It looks like I have to go fire a deputy and get back to work."

"I'm sorry you had to come home to this, Will."

"It's my job, Abe. What time do you have? I lost my watch."

Abe pulled out his pocket watch and flipped its lid. "Four fifty-five."

"Would you give Emma whatever she needs to make her comfortable. It looks like she might need to stay here a few nights while I take care of things. You know where I'll be."

"I'll take care of everything, Will."

"Thanks." He left the store and walked straight to his office. He found Radcliff sitting out front on the bench.

When Radcliff saw Will, he jumped to his feet. Wide-eyed, he said, "I didn't know you were back, sheriff!"

"I can see that, Radcliff. Why aren't you working, doing your rounds instead of just sitting here? There must be something you can do."

"I was just restin' for a bit, that's all."

"Well, I'm not going to beat around the bush. Please give me your badge. I'm going to have to fire you."

"But sheriff, Henry gave me this job!"

"But Henry isn't here, and I am. You're not qualified; that's why I said no last fall. Now give me your badge."

Radcliff pulled the badge from his shirt and slapped it in Will's hand and said, "Sheriff, it's not fair." He then walked away quickly, kicking the dirt as he went.

Will opened the door to his office to find it dirty and unkempt. Pulling open the drawers of the desk, he found them empty except the top right drawer, which held his pen and ink well along with a few pieces of paper. It was just as he had left it. The rack that once held the extra rifle was also void of its contents, and to top it off one of the two cell doors was open with keys in the lock. "What was Henry thinking?" he asked out loud. With a deep breath he pulled his badge from his shirt pocket and pinned it on.

He then grabbed the chair, sat down at the desk, and put his head down on his arms. "Lord," he said, "I'm tired, and I don't even have a deputy. I'll have no time to sleep being alone on this job. I need Your help and strength. Please be with me and make my burden light just as You have promised to do. Thank you, Jesus, amen."

After he had finished praying, he stood up, pushed the chair back, straightened his shirt, and headed out to start his rounds. He thought it best to let as many people as possible see him before dark, so he quickly walked the length of town from north to south, stopping at shops and stores along the way. He heard a number of complaints about the way things had been handled while he was gone and how they were glad he was back. Even the saloons where most of the trouble started had a few complaints, which were a bit unusual.

Watson at the livery stable bent his ear for a moment. It seemed that Henry was spending money much too freely for being a lawman. While Will was gone, Henry had purchased new boots, a new gun with a sharp holster, and some new clothes. He even had Watson re-shoe his horse and do some needed leather repair. More than likely the spending spree was due to his payoff from Lester. *It must have been a handsome sum*, Will surmised.

Back at his office he picked up the broom and swept it clean, but the one and only window was going to stay dirty for now. He left the door open and sat down on the bench greeting people as they passed. It was a pleasant sight to see Emma and his little sweetheart walking toward him with what looked like dinner. He stood to his feet and took Loretta into his arms, hugging her tightly.

"Let's go inside and sit at the desk. I brought food for us all," Emma said.

"What savory things did you bring, my dear?"

"Come inside and I'll show you." Emma reached into the large basket and started placing items on the desk—rolls, beets, carrots, early string beans, and baked beans, which Will loved. To finish off dinner, there was applesauce for a treat. Plates and silverware followed and were promptly put into place. They took their places and sat down.

"Let's pray." They bowed their heads and gave thanks. As they started to eat, Will noticed two men riding by the open door. It was the Atkin brothers he thought, but he let the thought pass. Family was his priority at this time. The two possible pests could wait.

"How is the town, Will?"

"Right now, quiet. I made my round and things looked good. Emma, there's one bit of bad news, though. Henry left town three nights ago. No one has seen him since, and nobody knows what he's up to. If he does come back, his job is no longer available. I'm seeing signs that he wasn't thinking clear. Some folks today have complained to me about him."

"Do you think he took to drinking?"

"No, he never was a drinker. I don't know what changed him, but a change did happen. He'd be better off if he didn't come back."

"Why would he leave? He had a good job, and you two worked well together. I don't understand."

"He has his reasons, hon. Maybe I'll have a chance to talk to him sometime. Anyway, I've been trying to figure out who could replace him, and then it dawned on me that Tanger would be a real asset to this town. When he gets here, I'm going to ask him to be my deputy."

"That sounds like a wonderful plan. Do you want more beans?"

"Yes." Just then a tall thin man poked his head in through the open door and interrupted their dinner. "Sorry, Sheriff, to be disturbing you and the misses, but I need to talk to you. It's real important."

"Give me a minute, Albert." He then turned to Emma. "I'm sorry to let work ruin our meal, but I need to see what's going on. I'll be right back."

When he stepped outside, he said firmly, "Now this better be important to take me away from my dinner."

"It is, sheriff. I think the Atkin brothers are planning something big. I can just tell. I've been watching them, and they sit around and do a lot of talking. I heard them say that if they had the chance they'd do it right away."

"Do what right away? I can't lock them up for talking, Albert. I'll tell you what, you keep an eye on them and report back to me if you hear anything of importance."

"I can do that, sheriff."

"I know you can, and thanks for the tip, Albert." He returned to dinner and finished eating in peace. Emma picked up the leftovers once they had finished, and she and Loretta strolled back to Abe's.

Will sat at his desk wondered how he was going to last through the night and whether Emma could handle what was to come. He couldn't shield her from the situation that had befallen them, but he believed in his heart that it had all transpired for a reason, and God held the reason. He sat like a stone statue deep in a world of his own that was traveling nowhere fast. The sun was on its way down, and the next scheduled rounds were calling him. Being the only lawman to carry the responsibilities was not glamorous—it wasn't even fun.

Fortunately, the homes and the shops that lined both sides of the town were quiet and peaceful. His last stop was his family. He moved up the stairs like a mouse and knocked on the wall. "Hi, I can only stay for a few minutes," Will stated as he sat down in the empty chair next to Emma at the table.

"I know you can't stay long, but I need to talk to you. Elizabeth and I were talking about our place, but I need more time, Will, before going home. The memories and my fears make it difficult. I'm just not ready yet. Elizabeth and Abe have offered us their second bedroom. Could we please accept their hospitality?"

"Yes, of course. I want what is best for you," Will replied softly.

"Thank you for understanding," she said as she hugged him tightly.

"My time is up. I need to head back. Thank you, Elizabeth, for sharing your place with us."

"I'd have it no other way, Mr. Sheriff," Elizabeth answered.

"If you need me, I'll be in my office or on Main Street." He lightly kissed Emma and headed for the door.

"Will, take these biscuits with you. They should hold you over for awhile," said Emma.

His walk down Main Street was uneventful, which pleased him. At the office he settled in for a long night of watching and waiting. Will attempted to fill a portion of the night with a few games of Solitare and picked up where he left off with a book he had started in the spring, but both of his efforts proved to be dissatisfying. His attitude had made a full circle, and he started to pray for the patience and peace that was needed.

He was amazed at how fast his sense of peace and trust could disappear when he looked to himself for strength and how quickly it returned when he repented and humbled himself before God. He said under his breath, "Lord, what is wrong with me? You gave Emma back to me, and You did it safely, and

I still have a lack of trust. Forgive me."

After confessing his lack of reliance on the Lord, he felt a strong impression to pour out his heart to Emma in a letter, expressing to her all that he was thankful for. After writing the letter, he fell asleep at his desk only to be awakened by a barking dog who was trying to chase away the rising sun.

Will took notice of the town once again. There was a tranquility that had fallen upon them, as if a cloud had overtaken them, and then one more token of God's love was displayed as Buckley made his appearance. "Good morning, Will. It looks like you've been here all night. I want you to go home to your family and not show up until tomorrow morning."

"I was told you were sick," Will replied.

"I was, but I'm well again. You know you can't run this town alone, so go home to your wife."

"I owe you one."

"You owe me one, all right. I just can't think of what it is right now."

"Thanks, Buckley." He walked to Abe's with a heart of gratitude.

Emma recognized Will's steps and met him on the landing. "An unexpected visit. How long can you stay?" she asked.

"Until seven in the morning. Buckley took over for me. He said he felt well again, and how could I turn down such an offer."

"That's exciting. Take off your gun and boots so you can relax. I'll get you a bite to eat." He did just that. After getting comfortable, he wandered down the hallway toward the sound of giggling and tittering. In the back bedroom he found Loretta playing dolls with Abe's daughter, and he gladly received his habitual hug and kiss before returning to eat.

"Will, I need to tell you what the Lord showed me."

"Please do."

"I believe He wants me to go home and face what happened, so He can heal me. The longer I hide the larger the fear will become, and He showed me a scripture that gave me peace. I'll read it to you."

Emma reached for her Bible. "It's found in Jeremiah 29:11 and 14: 'For I know the thoughts that I think toward you, says the Lord, thoughts of peace and not of evil, to give you a future and a hope. I will be found of you, says the Lord, and I will bring you back from your captivity; I will gather you from all the nations and from all the places where I have driven you, says the Lord, and I will bring you to the place from which I caused you to be carried away captive."

A sense of peace filled her soul again after reading the words. "Isn't it perfect? It's like it was written just for me."

"It seems so, honey, and I'm glad to have my captive back."

"We should go home in the next day or two."

"I'm happy to hear you say that. I know your faith is strong and the Lord will take care of our hearts, Emma. It's going to work out fine."

She patted the back of his left hand and said, "You know, Will Jacobs, you're a good man."

"I have to be for you because I love you so much."

She smiled though her eyes were wet—tears came easy these days. "How's the food, anyway?"

"I don't know. I haven't eaten any yet."

"Go ahead and eat, but listen to this. I have a new rhyme to share with you.

Air takes shape in the form of clouds
And drifts away without a sound
As I stand here upon the ground spellbound.

"That's what you saw when you looked up at the sky? I could never do that."

"Yep, that's what I saw in that big blue sky, and I was thinking about Christmas last night."

"It's a bit early, isn't it?"

"It's not about presents or the tree. I was thinking about the Baby Jesus in the manger, and since He's our Lord and Master, then He must be our 'Master in the Manger.' I want to compose a rhyme for that, but nothing has come to mind yet."

"Oh, something will, I'm sure."

Will took a few more bites of food before asking, "What would you like to do with the rest of the day?"

"Maybe go for a walk down by the creek."

"And on the way back we can stop at Martha's for a piece of her famous pie or whatever takes your fancy. Do you like the sound of that?" Will asked.

"Very much. When you're done, I'll get Loretta, and we'll be on our way," she said.

ૐૐૐૐૐૐ

The water level of the creek was perfect for wading and picking stones. Flowers dotted the banks with a variety of colors, and the birds shared their songs freely to any listening ear. It was a glorious day for the Jacobs family—the first outing since it all began. Loretta rode on her daddy's shoulders, pretending to be a giant picking leaves off the trees. The pie at Martha's did take their fancy along with the fresh lemonade. But they all agreed that the sunset was the icing on the cake to finish a perfect day.

Once back at Abe's and settled in for the night, Loretta gave her father a hug and said, "Daddy, would you read *The Little Girl Found a Pony* to me?"

"Yes, I will, and Abe, would you play your fiddle for us just like old times?"

"I've learned some new songs; I think you might enjoy them," Abe responded.

The music and friendship, blended with a large amount of laughter, filled up the evening and also filled their hearts, preparing them for a good night of rest.

The next morning Abe knocked firmly on the bedroom door to let Will know it was time to resume his duties and that his one-day vacation had ended. Emma dressed and joined him, Abe, and Elizabeth downstairs. The girls were still fast asleep. Time slipped away as the four friends visited, so a quick breakfast was all Will had time for, seeing that he had to relieve Buckley as scheduled.

"Good morning, Buckley. How'd things go?" Will asked.

"Peacefully. I've never seen the town like this."

"What you're seeing is an answer to my pray. I asked for God's help above and beyond what I already had, and He gave it to me."

"For me, seeing is believing, and I see it," Buckley stated.

"Did you do the rounds yet," Will asked.

"Less than a half hour ago. I found a window broken at Coleman's place, but that's it, Will."

"I'll report it to him later. You can take off and get some sleep. There's no need for you to hang around any longer. Thanks again for the help."

"You're welcome," Buckley said as left the office.

Will wrote out a request for a new rifle to replace the one that had disappeared when Henry did. He then stepped outside into the fresh air. He could tell that it was going to be a hot one. He started thinking about what he needed to do for the day. One of the things on his task list was a trip to Green Valley to set up a court date. Hopefully the judge would come to Stone Ridge for the trial because transporting the prisoners was a risk that he didn't want to take. *Tanger should be here any hour*, he thought. *I hope he's had a smooth trip. Everything is ready for the prisoners.*

The next few hours passed by slowly. With the town so peaceful, he found himself a little bored. He realized he needed some form of action to keep himself stimulated. It felt strange that the town could be almost too peaceful— he could see that his understanding of true peace was lacking. On his way back from the south end of town, he heard a storekeeper sternly say "You can't leave that wagon there. It's blocking my storefront."

"I'm sorry. I'm just stopping here for a few minutes," a familiar voice said.

Will spun around to see Tanger and Kate. "Tanger! Kate! Over here! Move your wagon in front of my office. It's six buildings down on the right. Am I glad to see you!"

Tanger dismounted Pik and approached Will. "Likewise, it's good to see you, too." Kate pulled ahead and stopped at the office; Joey following behind her as Max came running up to Will for a head rub.

"Where's Yann? I don't see him."

"He headed for San Francisco. He's hoping to find help to bring Sanne here."

"That doesn't surprise me."

"Are Lester and the others in the wagon?"

"You're not going to believe this, Will, but they're all dead."

"Did you shoot them?"

"No, they tried to escape at the fort. Peter and Lester were shot, but Allen died when his lungs gave out. I guess it was just a matter of time for him. They overpowered the guard, took his rifle, and ran, but they didn't get very far. No one else was hurt except the guard, and his injuries weren't too bad. It simplifies things for us here. There's no need for a trial or a hanging now. You know, Will, they would have hung."

"You're right; they would have. It's an odd kind of blessing, now Emma won't have to face them during the trial."

"Is Emma nearby, Will?" Kate interjected.

"She's just down the street with friends. Why don't we walk over and surprise her."

"Mr. Will, can I look inside your jail, please?"

"Not now, Clay, but you can later when we have more time. Maybe I'll even lock you up. How does that sound?" Will asked.

"Like fun! Would ya do that?"

"Yes, I will. Let's go see Emma," he said.

The walk was short, and so was the conversation. Entering Abe's store, they saw Elizabeth behind the counter. She looked up and said, "Will, are these the friends you've been waiting for?"

"Yes, Elizabeth. This is Tanger, Joey, Kate, and her son, Clay."

"It's nice to meet all of you. Emma has spoken highly of you. Let me get her." She walked to the stairway and called in a loud voice, "Emma, Kate and her family have arrived, please come down and see them."

Elizabeth then turned back to the waiting group. "I'm guessing it was a long trip. Are you hungry?"

"Yes," Clay and Tanger said in unison.

Emma appeared at the base of the stairs with obvious excitement. She quickly hugged each one of them but lingered with Joey. He held a special place in her heart that no one else could hold. A flood of memories from the previous weeks engulfed her as she saw her friends.

"My leg is better," Joey said, pulling up his pant leg and pointing to his wound.

The groups chatted about their trip and recent events. Elizabeth soon excused herself to go prepare food for their guests.

"Tanger, would you walk back to the office with me? We need to talk," Will said. "Abe, I'll see you later. We'll be back in a few minutes so that Tanger can eat and get a little rest."

The two men headed out the door and turned to walk down the street. They had walked past two storefronts before Will shared what was on his mind. "Tanger, when I got back Henry, my deputy, was gone, so I'm working alone with a little help from Buckley, a man you'll soon meet."

"It looks like you're in a pickle. Let me guess—you want me to be your new deputy. Is that what this little talk is about?"

"Yeah, I need your help, and I'd love to have you stay in the area, but I don't know what your plans are now that our little adventure is over."

"Well, Kate and I have talked in depth, and we've decided that we don't want a long courtship. We're actually planning on getting married real soon. We haven't decided where to settle, but when we pulled into town, Kate said she liked the looks of the place already, so it looks as if I'm stayin' for awhile."

"Is that a yes to the job?"

"It's a yes to the job. I've never been a lawman before, so I might need a little education."

"That I can provide, deputy! Step into your new office, and I'll pin a badge on you."

"By the way, what's my pay per month? I'm going to have a family soon, you know."

"Seventy-five dollars a month. It's not the best or worst, but it puts food on the table. You can stay with us for a time, if you like."

Will pinned a badge on Tanger's shirt. "It looks good on you. Now it's time for the town to meet you," Will said.

Once outside Wayne O'Connell flagged them down. "Sheriff, it's the Atkin brothers again. They were in my store just a few minutes ago causing trouble. They were fresh to one of my lady customers and to Betty, and on top of that, I watched them take a small tin of dried fruit worth three dollars. After leaving my store, they walked over to the saloon. Take care of this problem, sheriff, would you!"

"O'Connell, my new deputy and I will take care of it right now."

"Thanks, sheriff," he said as he turned and ran back across the street to his store.

Will and Tanger quickly walked over to the saloon and stopped outside. "Tanger, I want you to wait by the door as I go in and try to reason with them. You'll know when to come in."

Once inside Will saw two good-sized men standing at the bar. As he approached them, the one nearest him slid something across the bar. Will grabbed it and quickly discovered that it was the empty tin from the dried fruit. "If I'm correct, you two are the Atkin brothers?" He then stepped back, giving himself plenty of room.

"That's right, we are. And you're the sheriff I suppose."

"Yesterday I had complaints about you two men, and this morning a townsperson registered another complaint. So let's cut to the chase. You can put the three dollars on the bar for the fruit you took from O'Connell's store, and I'll consider it paid for, or I'll lock you both up. If you'll stop disturbing the peace, we'll get along just fine; if not, the same consequences will result— I'll lock you both up."

"Sheriff, you look like you took a good beating once, and if you try to lock us up, you'll get another one, and maybe it will be worse than your last one."

"That remains to be seen. This is your last chance. Put the money on the bar."

The two brothers stepped apart, and the taller one said, "No, sheriff, I won't."

Upon hearing that Tanger made his move. "Say, brother, are you having trouble? Would you like my help?"

"Yeah, I would. You two haven't met my big brother, have you? We're a close family, and he doesn't like anybody bothering his little brother."

Tanger stepped forward in front of Will and made eye contact with the Atkin brothers. He then spoke in a friendly tone, "Boys, why don't you put the money on the bar and go home. That would make us real happy, and don't be causing any more problems in our town because we *will* lock you up."

"Roy, I think we should be smart and do as they say." He pulled three dollars from his pocket, placed it on the bar, and walked out, leaving Roy standing alone with Will and Tanger. Roy quickly determined that being alone and having to face these two lawmen was not something he wanted to do, so he took his brothers advice and left peacefully.

"You handled that wisely. I think you're a natural," Will said.

"That was easy. They're not tough; they just like to think so. We won't hear much from them anymore."

"Come on, deputy. I'll show you the rest of the town."

Chapter Ten

Life's Second Chance

The weeks flew by, and Emma, Will, Tanger, and Kate settled into a pleasant routine. The men enjoyed working together, and Emma and Kate spent their days out at the Jacobs place gardening, sewing, cleaning, and tending to the children. In the evenings Tanger always came to call if he were not on duty in town. They often spent time together as a foursome, enjoying each others company and talking about their day.

The more time they spent together, the more clearly it was that Tanger and Kate were meant to be together. They fit together so perfectly, and before long Tanger proposed and Kate accepted.

Will and Emma were so happy for their friends, and Emma didn't waste any time in organizing some of her women friends in town to help plan the wedding. Although it would be a small affair, Emma wanted it to be a special celebration for her dear friends.

Before they knew it, the big day finally arrived. It was a Sunday, and the Lord had provided a clear blue sky with a slight breeze that tempered the rays of the sun, making it a pleasant day for the wedding. It was shortly before noon, and all fifteen of the guests and participants had arrived and were milling around visiting.

Emma and Elizabeth had decorated the banisters and posts of the front porch of Will and Emma's home for the wedding. They had gathered wild flowers of pinks, blues, and yellows with a few reds added in—it was simple, yet tastefully done. For the reception, they would be serving fresh apple and peach pies that had been provided by some of the ladies and Martha's restaurant and punch. They also had baked a small wedding cake. Everything was ready; they were just waiting on Tanger.

"The groom should be here any moment, I hope," Abe commented to Will. "Kate won't come down, and neither will our wives until he arrives, does he know that?" he said a little impatiently.

"Tanger is just being Tanger. He headed to Main Street more than an hour ago and said he'd be back soon. I know that Pastor Reynolds wants to start on time." Will looked around and then exclaimed, "There he is! Look behind you, Abe; he's tying up his horse under the oak tree."

"Look at the new man with new pants and—"

Tanger cut Abe off. "Don't look at me like that. It wasn't my idea."

"Kate is going to love the new you, Tanger," Will said with a grin.

"The new me! This is just temporary."

"Tanger, Pastor Reynolds would like your presence on the porch. We're about to start, and Abe, that means you, too. Grab your fiddle please," said Eugene, one of the believers from the house church.

"Ladies and gentlemen, we're going to start shortly. I was just informed that the bride is ready to make her appearance as soon as we are all in position, so let's not keep her waiting. Sheriff, you stand here to the right of Mr. Tanger. Now your bride, Mr. Tanger, will come through the door and down the steps and take her place to your left. I'm going to stand off to your right until she's at your side, then I'll take my place on the third step and of course your wife, sheriff, will follow the bride and stand to her left."

"Sheriff, do you have the rings?"

"Yes, I do."

"Abe, could you play something appropriate before we begin?" the pastor asked.

Abe nodded his head and started a sweet melody.

The pastor stuck his head in the doorway, then turned, and said, "She's coming. Everyone quiet, please." Abe shifted from his sweet melody to the awaited wedding march. The soon-to-be Mrs. Tanger appeared in the doorway. She smiled as Tanger raised his left hand, motioning her to him. She wore a cream-colored, short-sleeved cotton dress with just a touch of white lace. Her nearly mid-back length hair had been braided and wrapped atop her head then finished with a half dozen white daises.

She carried a small bouquet that had been fashioned from the same flowers that decorated the porch. She took her place at Tanger's side and admired his clean-shaven face, for he had a handsome and masculine look about him that pleased her.

They both looked toward Pastor Reynolds as he said, "Ladies and gentlemen, before they are joined in marriage, I would like to say a few things. I felt impressed to study the topic of marriage in a way that I never have before in preparation for this service, and I'd like to share some of these new insights with you. I'm hoping that this short talk will be beneficial to the married and the unmarried as well.

"Marriage is not just a contract between a man and a woman. It's a covenant between God and husband and wife. God Himself instituted it at Creation, making it a holy union that was to be set apart from all other relationships. And this marriage relationship was meant to be a safe haven on earth to protect the family. The home can be a place of peace and joy where kind, loving words are spoken, where respect and acceptance is given. A God-centered marriage can protect its members from the ungodly effects of this world and can lay a wonderful foundation for the children, for no parent wants rebellious unruly children.

"Now, if the husband is the head of the household, what advice can I give to you men besides what has already been given to you? Husbands, you must forsake all others in thought and feelings and also with your eyes, because you can't serve two women just like you can't serve God and this world. The Word of God says, 'Husbands, love your wives, just as Christ also loved the church and gave Himself for her.' Not only did our Lord take great abuse for us, He also died for us. So husbands, give yourselves unreserved to your wives, and let your children know that you love and care for them. Reveal to them how important they are to you. Love begets love.

"I would like to address the ladies at this time. Ladies, an excellent wife is the crown of her husband, and the man who finds a wife finds a good thing and obtains favor from the Lord. Ladies, can two walk together unless they are in agreement? So agree on everything that you possibly can, and when you can't, treat your husband with respect. Men, this is meant for you also. All of us should be more thankful and rejoice more together. I want all of us to consider the quality of life we could share if we all followed these guidelines within our families and with friends and strangers.

"Eric and Kate, the time has come that you, along with your friends, have been waiting for. Your guests are about to witness two lives become one. Please do not take this union lightly. Let no one interfere in the smallest of ways with this holy covenant between the Lord and yourselves.

"You have come here today to proclaim before God and friends your love and commitment to each other, and to your soon-to-be son, Clay. Eric if you desire Clay to be an upright son, then you yourself must strive to be an upright man and you will be richly rewarded. Eric, I'm going to speak forthright to you. Your choice in taking Kate as your bide was wise; I can see her love for you. But as time passes situations will arise that will try your love and patience as if you were both iron rubbing against one another.

"At those times you may be tempted to think that you married the wrong women, but don't fall for that because it's a lie of the devil. Today you are making a covenant with God, those two pieces of iron, if worked rightly, can become smooth and durable. Never lose sight of your love for her and the reason for taking her as your wife.

"Kate, my words to you as a preacher of the Word of God is to love him, love him, love him and let no situation steal your faith in your heavenly Father. Be steadfast and unmovable when your faith is tried.

"It is now time to start your vows. Eric Tanger, do you take Kate Weissman to be your lawfully wedded wife, and do you promise and covenant before God and these witnesses to be a loving and faithful husband, in plenty and in want, in joy and in sorrow, in sickness and in health, to honor and protect, to lay down your life to preserve hers, if necessary, for as long as you both shall live, so help you God?"

"Yes, I do," he said with deep conviction as he gazed into her eyes.

"You may place the ring on her finger," Pastor Reynolds stated.

Tanger took the ring from Will and carefully placed it on her finger. "I love you, Kate," he said.

"Now, Kate Weissman, do you take Eric Tanger to be your lawfully wedded husband, and do you promise and covenant before God and these witnesses to be a loving and faithful wife, to honor and cherish him in plenty and in want, in joy and in sorrow, in sickness and in health for as long as you both shall live, so help you God?"

"Yes, with all my heart, I do."

"Please place the ring on his finger, Kate," he said.

She did so with a smile that said many things.

"Mr. Tanger, you may now kiss your bride," Pastor Reynolds said lightheartedly.

Their friends burst forth with clapping as they sealed the ceremony with their kiss.

"Ladies and gentlemen, I present to you Mr. and Mrs. Eric Tanger. Come, welcome them and let us enjoy the festivities." As everyone gathered around, sweet music could once again be heard drifting on the air. A few minutes later Elizabeth's voice was heard announcing that pie was ready to be served in the house and that the wedding cake would be cut in due time. Kate whispered in Eric's ear to invite everyone into the house to continue the party.

"My bride would like us all to move into the house to continue the celebration, and I, for one, would like a piece of that pie."

At that moment Tanger felt Clay's arms around his waist, and he heard him say, "Now you're my pa, aren't you?"

"Yes, I am, son."

Hearing that made Clay hug him all the tighter.

As they passed Abe, who was playing his fiddle, Tanger said, "Take a break and join us inside for pie. The food has gotten everyone's attention."

Everyone was enjoying their pie and other treats. Some were sitting while others stood in the small front room. Most of the windows were open, letting the breeze move through the house and making the gathering quite comfortable. The mood of the reception was jovial. A number of people commenting about how beautiful Kate looked and about how perfect and God-centered the whole ceremony had been.

As everyone mixed and mingled, a few women stole Kate away, asking her about present and future plans. Tanger spotted Will across the room and headed his way. He was stopped once or twice to receive congratulatory comments—his new friends were gracious and thankful for him accepting the deputy position. These men were of the opinion that Otis had been an embarrassment to the town and that Tanger was a great improvement. Tanger caught Will on his way toward Emma with a plate of pie in each hand.

"Will."

"Yes, Mr. Tanger, what may I do for you on your glorious wedding day?"

"Thanks for the house and everything. It won't be easily forgotten."

"I believe you'd do the same for me, and where is your bride? Did you lose her already? She's a keeper, you know."

"Yeah, I figured that out on my own. She was grabbed by some women who had a few questions about future plans and the like."

"Go win her back and bring her over to the front, I'll keep two chairs open for you."

Tanger put his left hand on Will's right shoulder. "First I need to say something, Will. My given name is Eric Isaac Tanger. Tanger doesn't feel right anymore. I'm starting a new life, so I'd appreciate it if you would call me Eric from here on."

"I'm happy that you have peace over it, Eric, and I'll gladly comply. Now go get Kate and enjoy the rest of this day with her."

They both disappeared in opposite directions.

The afternoon passed quickly as if the hands of the clock were moved by the touch of the invisible. It tends to be that way, especially when one desires the occasion to linger on, to be thoughtfully absorbed, to be captured for that future moment when life becomes hard and trying or just for a pleasant memory.

The reception was thinning out as friends said their goodbyes. Elizabeth and Emma, along with their husbands, hurriedly put the house in order and made their exit, leaving the newlyweds to the peace and joy of their new beginnings. The Lord had placed them in each other's path, and now He would mold them into a strong family that would withstand the pressures of life and be an influence for good.

As the two couples and the kids arrived at Abe's, the children ran off to play in the backyard, leaving the adults to themselves. Since the store was closed, the remainder of sunlight could be spent at their leisure, which didn't happen that often seeing the ages of their combined children.

"I know you have to take over for Buckley later, but do you have plans until then?" Abe asked Will curiously.

"I was going to ask Emma to take a ride with me down to the creek for awhile," Will replied.

"I'd like that. We could sit under that shade tree near the water and soak our feet," Emma said with a sense of excitement in her voice.

"Do you mind if Loretta and Clay stay behind with Molly until we get back?" Will asked.

"No, that's fine. Go and enjoy some time together. You need it."

The creek was serene along with its surroundings. They found themselves under their favorite shade tree, and they couldn't have asked for a time more suited to be alone together. The sunlight was reflecting off of the water—it had a similarity to a jeweled sequenced dress that Emma had once seen in a store window in San Francisco. It was beautiful.

"You've been so quiet, dear, since we left Abe's. What's on your mind," Emma asked kindly.

"The things I need to say, I need to say just so. You know at times it's hard for me to put my feelings into words."

"Do the best you can. I certainly want to know what's on your mind, so please tell me."

"Since we got back, Emma, I've been preoccupied with my job, trying to make this town as safe as possible. I don't want you or Loretta to suffer like that ever again or anything close to it. What I've done by trying to protect you is to neglect you both. Today Pastor Reynolds' words reached me. When he said 'Husbands, love your wives even as Christ loved the church and gave Himself for her' that was all I needed to hear. The time I've spent with Loretta has been very little and with you really not much more. I'm sorry. Please forgive me and help me with this."

Emma hugged him tightly and then stretched out on the ground, placing her head in his lap. She looked up at him and said, "My dear, that's not much to forgive you for, but I do forgive you. You were only doing what you thought to be the best for us. I can't fault you for that or complain about the love and care you give because there's plenty of that. There are a lot of women in this world who would enjoy being cared for as you care for us.

"There must be a balance that we can find between your job and us. I believe the Lord would have it that way. Do you think that the town council would agree to add another deputy? Perhaps Buckley would accept the position. He already fills in for you. It would be nice to have you around more often."

"That's a good idea. I didn't think of that. I'll talk to a few town councilmen tomorrow and see how they feel about it. Maybe Buckley would consider the job. You're a pretty smart woman, Emma. I like having you around."

"You'd better! Is it all right to change the direction of this conversation?" she asked.

"Yes, it is."

"It's concerning Eric and Kate. Where are they going to live after their honeymoon?"

"Maybe it will never end. We may have lost our house and inherited Clay as our son," Will said laughing.

"Ha ha! Be serious," she said as she poked him in the ribs.

"OOOOuch."

"That didn't hurt. In all seriousness, do you know of any place for them to live?"

"No, but I can add it to the list."

"Thank you. It's important to me that they have a comfortable place to call home."

"Emma, I could put my head back against this tree and take a nap."

"Go ahead for a little while. I'll lie here and absorb the peace and quiet."

"Don't let me sleep too long."

"Relax, my dear, I won't let you be late. Do I get a kiss first?"

"Yes."

"I thought so," she said.

In the quietness of the afternoon, a thankful heart and a prayerful attitude came easy to Emma. After surviving the kidnapping and returning to her family and home, every day had become a gift. She could write a list a yard long of the tokens of God's love that He had poured out on her. The scripture that she had heard and read more than once had taken on a new meaning for her: "And we know that all things work together for good to those who love God, to those who are called according to His purpose."

If it wasn't for the storm that almost swept her away, the healing from the past would not have taken place. Also, the growth in faith and trust in God and the deepening relationship with her husband and daughter were an outgrowth of this healing process.

She was lying so still that a small song bird she had seen from time to time but couldn't attach a name to landed on the toe of her shoe. It sang a song as it fluffed its feathers before flying off to a branch of a nearby tree. How she wished it would've stayed for a time so she could fill her eyes with the fine details of its feathers and colors, but it was still a thrill even for the moment.

Realizing that their afternoon jaunt was coming to a close, Emma plucked a blade of grass and began to tickle Will's nose and cheek. He soon opened his eyes. "Hi, we should go now," she said.

Emma stood to her feet and brushed off a few leaves and grass from her dress. She then reached for the sky with a tall stretch. "Do you feel refreshed? I do. It's so peaceful here. Wouldn't it be a wonderful thing if we could build a house right on this spot with the porch facing the creek? Then we could make a path to its edge and line it with flowers. I can see it now. It's so nice to dream, isn't it?" Emma mused.

"If we did that I'd never go back to work. I'd just stay here with my beautiful bride and little girl and live in your dream, and I'd probably enjoy it. And to answer your question, Yes, I am a bit rested. If I need help tonight, could you come and take over for awhile?"

"Certainly, my dear. I shall protect this town fearlessly with my knitting needles, and my fame will spread far and near. But then I'd be asked to replace you, and you don't want to be without employment, so I think it wiser that I stay at home tonight. Would you agree?"

"Thank you for being so thoughtful of my feelings and my standing in this community. It's so kind of you," he said with a wink.

"You're welcome, my dear," Emma said, returning his playful look.

"Now let's go before I'm late."

As they climbed into the wagon and headed off, she asked, "If I bring you a meal around eight, would that satisfy you?"

"Yes, it would, but if I'm not there, don't wait very long. You can leave it on the desk because I never know when I'll be back, as you well know."

As they rode past the blacksmith's shop, Joey could be seen out front rubbing the neck of his newly acquired white and brown Paint Horse. Will had assisted him in working out a deal with Watson, the blacksmith, for it, which Joey quickly renamed Shasta because her white face reminded him of Mount Shasta. It was in answer to Emma's prayer that the Lord had provided work for Joey. Watson welcomed the opportunity to have a man with such strength and an obvious gift with horses.

The deciding factor had been somewhat of a challenge. Watson told Joey that if he could bring in the stallion that was out in the coral and tie him up to the post so Watson can shoe him, then Joey could have the job. Watson had been trying for two days without a bit of success to catch the stallion. Joey quietly accepted the challenge, and after calmly and gently coaxing the stallion, he had the animal subdued and under his control; thus the job was his. The job included a small room that was accessed from the stable—it was perfect for Joey, considering his great love for the four-legged beasts. He slept more soundly each night knowing that the horses under his care were safely bedded down.

Will kissed Emma goodbye and climbed down from the wagon. Entering the office he saw Buckley with his nose stuck in some paperwork. "I see you had a little trouble. What crime did he commit?" Will asked referring to the man in the cell.

"I locked him up for causing a fight at the saloon, but there was some property damage, so I've imposed a fine to cover the damages. I thought he'd cool down easier here than there."

"Could I interrupt you for a minute and talk to you outside?"

"Sure, I can finish this after."

Will explained his idea for expanding the sheriff's office and asked Buckley if he'd be interested in a full-time position. Buckley said he'd consider it, but would need a little time to make a decision.

ও০০ও০০ও০০ও০

The next three days were momentous. The pesky drunk was released from his cell only to be put back for more of the same. The Town Council surprisingly responded much quicker than Will had anticipated, giving him approval to hire Buckley as his second deputy, and Buckley accepted the offer, stating that he'd be honored to hold the position. The only cog in the wheel was that the Town Council voted not to support him in the next town election. They wanted a sheriff who would be totally committed to the job without any reservations. Emma's comment on the council's new direction and change of heart was that if God allowed this job to dry up then He would provide something else. She wasn't shaken by it.

Eric returned from his honeymoon with a glow that was obvious to most. He was full of enthusiasm for what the future held. As Will watched him go about his rounds, he marveled at what love could do for a soul. Soon after their return, Eric and Kate found a house for rent on Oak Wood Street on the west side of town. Will thought it was a good move, for he reasoned that to have a lawman living in that area of town could be a positive influence.

Most of life's pieces were fitting together nicely. Except for the scars and the undesirable memories that they had to deal with over time, life was a blessing. The one fear that followed Emma from day to day was the fear of being alone, especially while she was at home where it had all begun. Emma understood that scars heal and memories fad, but it was hard work, and at times the hardest thing to do was not to run to Will or to a friend when that fear overtook her.

When she was seized with fear, she felt as if her body had a mind of its own and wanted to run away without permission. At those times she would break out in a sweat as a flood of memories paralyzed her. Emma had considered moving away, away from the reminders, but that would also remove her from the life she and Will had built there in Stone Ridge. The paralyzing effects of her fear also left her confused at times. Will and her close friends could only comfort her so much, which left her with just one place to go and that was to Jesus, to the only One who can give true healing to the heart and mind.

No matter how painful it was for her to work her way through the remnants of the kidnapping, she knew that Jesus was by her side.

She was reminded of the words "For our light afflictions, which is but for a moment, is working for us a far more exceeding and eternal weight of glory. The Lord's lovingkindness and watchful eye is never ending, for He neither slumbers nor sleeps. For it would be inconsistent with His character to be anything other than who He is and what has already been proclaimed, 'Wonderful, Counselor, Mighty God, Everlasting Father, Prince of Peace.'

He lives to give and to bless; He loves to do good to us with all His heart."

As Emma worked to close a chapter on her life and lay to rest the most terrifying experience of her life, she was inspired to pen these words:

Oh, what would I do without You?
Without the love You gave,
the way You cared,
this life You spared,
the promise You'd be here.

Oh, what would I do without You?
It scares me just to think,
the guilt, the shame,
a life of pain,
the wounds that will not heal.

Oh, what would I do without You?
I'd simply cease to be,
I could not sing,
I would not bring,
the praises of Your love.

Oh, what would I do without You?
 Without the love You gave.

We invite you to view the complete
selection of titles we publish at:

www.ASPECTBooks.com

Scan with your mobile
device to go directly
to our website.

or write or email us your praises,
reactions, or thoughts about this
or any other book we publish at:

ASPECT Books

www.ASPECTBooks.com

P.O. Box 954
Ringgold, GA 30736

info@ASPECTBooks.com

ASPECT Books titles may be purchased in bulk for
educational, business, fund-raising, or sales promotional use.
For information, please e-mail:

BulkSales@ASPECTBooks.com.

Finally, if you are interested in seeing
your own book in print, please contact us at

publishing@ASPECTBooks.com.

We would be happy to review your manuscript for free.